Alicia Cahalane Lewis

RESTLESS

ALICIA CAHALANE LEWIS is a ninth-generation Quaker from the Shenandoah Valley of Virginia. She holds an MFA in creative writing from Naropa University where her poetry appeared in *Not Enough Night.* She is the author of *nebulous beginnings and strings* (Tattered Press, 2017), featuring art by Shenandoah Valley artist Winslow McCagg. Her chapbook, *The Fish Turned the Waters Over so the Birds Would Have a Sky,* a contemplative meditation on the origins of evolution, was published by The Lune Chapbook Series (Spring, 2017). *The Intrepid Meditator* (2021), a self-help memoir, and the accompanying novella, *Room Service Please* (2022), were published by Tattered Script Publishing. A Reiki Master, Alicia continues to live and work in the Shenandoah Valley.

aliciacahalanelewis.com

RESTLESS

To Bay:

There is no other
recourse but a memory.

♡

[signature]

Restless

Alicia Cahalane Lewis

Tattered Script Publishing

Tattered Script Publishing
PO Box 1704
Middleburg, Virginia 20117
tatteredscript.com

ISBN 9781737521945 (hardcover)
ISBN 9781737521952 (ebook)
Printed in the United States of America
10 9 8 7 6 5 4 3 2 1

Tattered Script Publishing: Crafting Cultural Creativity and Authenticity

Cover art and design by Emily Kallick

First Printing 2023

For my daughter, Sarah, with love

What wisdom can you find that is greater than kindness?
Jean-Jacques Rousseau

One

Emilie

There is nothing to be afraid of. Love is a stereoscope of emotional pictures in the mind. And the mind, rummaging around and through love, complicates the heart. And then the heart cries. It weeps. Love is a complex set of emotions I never thought I would be able to understand, that is until I met you.

I do not normally engage in conversations I feel threatened by. I pull out of situations that make me uncomfortable. I do not react well to strangers, and because you are perceived to be a stranger I feel noticeably unhinged by your presence.

The boulevard is dotted with dappled light. You come to me in this abstract way, the whole of you invisible until I lift my eyes and gaze upon your battered soul. You hide behind a waistcoat, your breast a peacock blue, and I notice that the gold pocket watch is neither elaborate nor sentimental. This mystifies me. You walk upright, as fashionable men walk in the early evening, with your top hat securely in place, and neither my sorry eyes nor my threadbare skirt diverts the gaze you have upon these wilted flowers. It is the flowers you want. I am no one. My skirt is unfashionable thereby making me a vagabond and you, the reason I must live.

––––––––––

The streets of Paris are antiquated, although there are new electric lamps on the Avenue de l'Opéra to liven the dreary moods of those who live inside her columned vestibules. But I am not certain you are as well-heeled as your polished boots make you appear to be, and I wonder now if your vestibule has columns. I know mine did. Once.

I walk behind you, your gloved hand smartly carrying a bouquet of unopened roses, and I follow the shadows your feet make on the cobblestone street as you sidestep horse manure and mud. My hallowed boots are cracked and absorb smells. I once walked in puddles and disregarded it all. Until now. I remember to be careful where I place my feet. Careful, so that should you invite me in to dine with you I will be clean. I have nowhere to go. I once had a fashionable house, a maman, and a papa who brought me sweetness, and there was nothing to ever want. I am no longer that child, for I ran away from this long ago. I now have needs.

I notice the stained glass window, now cracked, and you notice perhaps the tarnished handle of your apartment door, but you do not look up at the glass as you enter. Your gloved hand, covered smartly in gray felt, is ever so slightly stained. You seem to appreciate the sudden warmth, but you struggle to close the wooden door against the wind. And it is in this moment that you lift your dark eyes, diverted momentarily from the pleasures of your room, to look at me. I thought I had been long gone from a realm such as this, but should you invite me in to dine I would hold a silver spoon and sip my soup just as you do.

———

It never occurs to me that you might have a wife. After all, there are roses. Red. I struggle against the darkening day. I have nowhere promising to go. I could turn and run, as I am inclined to, and push my narrow boots across an abstraction such as this life. I could promise myself nothing, and believe in nothing, but nothing is as complicated as something. I know I should have taken the taffy Papa gave me and enjoyed its sweetness, but I turned on him as I must turn on you.

I am no longer a child. I know nothing a child knows. I have my memories, but they are incomplete vestiges of a by-gone era when I was taken around the pebbled parks of Paris in a barouche so we could be seen. My maman sat upon stiff brocade and I, tipped in mink from head to toe, sat stoically stone-faced. There is no other recourse, but a memory, for Maman and Papa died and have long ago been buried. I have outgrown my past and have thrown the tattered aubergine wool coat and hat, a fashionable child's bonnet, away. I turned on my brother Henri and tossed my wealth aside when what I had was way too much.

Do I make myself and the picture postcards of my life clear? I grew up in want of nothing. I would come in from a windy walk such as this, my blonde hair curled and tied up in ribbons, my boots polished, and be greeted at the door. I entertained myself by a fire such as you are going to do. Where is your man to answer the door? Have you a wife?

You stop momentarily when you look upon me and gasp. I am a heathen for sure, but I am old enough to know I can get away with this childlike innocence. I push the fraying cap off my head to show you the golden stubble of lopped-off curls. I give all that is left of the curls to the winter wind so that the lamp will show you just how my gold beckons. There are some who move their feet as though in all of life there is a dance. I move my tousled hair in ways I imagine those who have taken to the prairie move theirs. At least I feel that their lives should afford them tousled hair and wind.

I once saw a picture postcard of the American West and imagined myself living there. I wanted to roll up the sleeves of my dirty muslin, take off my sunbonnet, and let the wind carry me as a tumbleweed across my unintended existence. In the West, I would have a maman, a papa, and a brother who would pioneer their rugged souls alongside mine. We would travel as a brave and studious family into uncharted realms. We would go where no one had dared to go before, conquering our fear of rattlesnakes and vermin.

———————

There is nothing easy about the windy streets of Paris, especially at night. I toss what is left of my tangled hair and you grimace. You close the door and now you are behind a panel I cannot see into or through. There are curtains at your apartment window, perhaps double-lined to protect you from the cold. I wear a soiled but once-opulent gentleman's dark opera cape and a pair of mismatched riding gloves. If you were foolish enough to drop a glove, and I know not if one of these was yours (as much as I would love for it to be), I was clever enough to pick it up. I have a smart collection of misplaced gloves: dark leather, flannel, silk, suede, fingerless, frayed woolen mittens, and a child's lavender kidskin with a single pearl button. Extremely rare.

I run my hands down the shrunken summer skirt of dusty rose and tug on the parcel to make sure my gloves are still there. I wear a tattered wool petticoat for warmth in the winter and carry it in the silk parcel in the summer, but the mismatched gloves have become something of a talisman. I feel as though I must carry them with me, always, for protection. I pull uneasily on the soiled skirt, and despite the cold sharp air, I unbutton the fraying collar of my flannel shirtwaist. It will not suit in a few months. I have grown and begun to fill out. My hips are not as narrow and my breasts are not as lean.

The wind carries with it the scent of something newly cut crackling on a vigorous fire. There are wet branches of some kind that you have tossed, without thinking, and they smoke. I hear you cough. I strain to listen for the pitter-patter of children's feet, the chime of a grandfather clock announcing the hour, and a bell to tell you it is time to dress for dinner, but the house is quiet. I cannot imagine a wife. I feel it in every part of my being that I am yours and when I knock upon the door, and you answer, you will lock your wondrous eyes upon mine and then in all seriousness complain that I am too modern and must never go about the streets alone. You will take me into your arms, hold me against your heart, and I will soften and promise you I have no need for independence.

———————

The wind shifts direction and brings with it a frozen spitting rain. I am without an umbrella, or anything, really, to divert the misery. But this is what I know: I am orphaned. I haven't a warm fire to go home to. I once had these pleasures, but they are now lost. I pause and stare into the crimson light that bleeds profusely from behind the open curtains. They are red. The papered walls are red. Your wife loves red. Or is it your mother? I have a hard time imagining that you have decorated your apartment yourself, but one never knows these days. We are between knowing.

Uneasily, you close the curtains. I can only imagine your tall trim body, your slender hand on the varnished fireplace mantle, and a nod to your lover behind this veil, for the dusty curtains are too thick to make your movements known to me. I must imagine. You are a gentleman to buy my flowers. And when you took them from me you never once looked into me as I looked into you. You put the centime into my frozen hand and watched the petals bend. I know you wanted to protect them for the someone you love, and so when you turned from me I followed. I want to know your love.

The streets are busy now with evening travelers and I am getting kicked about with mud from the wheels of their horse-drawn carriages. I hesitate to leave you, for if I do, and turn my back, I know I will wound myself once more. I was born to greater wealth than you. I lost it. I could have found perhaps temporary comfort with my aunt Élodie, but she was cruel, or so I thought. I had read too many harrowing tales of cruelty, and I knew that once she took Maman's money, as all vain aunts are want to do, especially in the stories I had read, she would throw me out upon the grate. So to spare her the newfound richness of her grieving heart, or is that the poverty, I stole away into the night and never said goodbye.

I am sure Henri was sent to live in an impoverished house for wayward souls and had I stayed with him I would have accompanied him. Or I would have been sent away to school, and given a uniform and a matching coat. Or taken into another home and given perfectly harmless chores to do. I know not. Had I not run from home would we have met some other way?

I have dreamt of this life. In it, I am sitting by an electric lamp taking stock of all I am. I do not want. I have a fire. Your love. We have a child. Had I stayed with my brother who knows where I would be? Perhaps my aunt would have taken pity on us and let us stay with her in Maman's great house. She would have employed an even finer governess and dressed us up in her gaudy ways. But the house was sold, and I am certain my brother was stripped of his name and shipped off, and I, as a result of my childish ways, have been left behind to walk the streets alone.

In my mind, my brother is somewhere just as negligible

as these windy streets, but I do not know. I know nothing of his whereabouts, and over time, as I have grown accustomed to myself I fear that should I ever see him I would find him changed. I would not know him and he would not know me. No face of his would look familiar for he was but four years old and I, eleven, when our maman and papa were taken to their God.

In her spectacular demise of character, yes quite a character flaw, my feral aunt, once suited for a lesser rung, now wears my mother's diamond brooch. I have seen her parade about the streets dragged down by Maman's mink, but there is nothing I can do about it. She abandoned me at the time I needed her most. I do not want her or my mother's jewels. I do not need her fur. I close the stolen cape around me tightly, and in doing so remember Maman, but it is not a happy memory. I never understood nor will I ever understand her love. I know I confused her. No, let me be more clear. I compounded the fears she had about herself and there is nothing more to say. She did not want children. She preferred the scene to be something of another silhouette where men are lovers uninterrupted by impatient childish squeals.

When it was hers to take, Maman took her mother's money and spent it freely. Against Papa's wishes, she gambled at roulette and won enough to buy a house so that before I was brought into this world she became known for her great wealth. She hid the gambling.

It is my late mother's riches, she would say, and no one suspected the truth. But I knew. Papa was beside himself with guilt and anguished greatly.

Servants talk, he would whisper, then tie his silk tie tighter and do nothing about it, too weak or ineffectual, I guess, to go against her.

For this, I find him just as cruel. How does an eager man become weak? And how, I fear, will I ever understand Maman's penchant for more? Had she been found out, no one would have accepted us in that inner circle of old wealth. She would have been thrown to the street to scavenge. But before she was found to be a fraud, as I am certain as fleas in my bed that she would have been, Maman and Papa died in a train car accident. I have come to the streets of Paris a pauper with her secret still intact.

I made the choice to flee. I look back on this time and it is as clear as glass. There are no irregular shadows. I see the vibrancy of the moonlit night and the golden lamps upon the street just as I did the night I ran away. I still walk the avenues and beg. I steal. I take what is mine to take and offer whatever I can in its place. Perhaps some part of me wanted to know the streets the way a gypsy knows the streets, and so as one of those wayward characters in Maman's novels, I took her to the streets to know. I guess you could say I wanted what I could not have just as Maman wanted what was beyond her reach. She put on a costume, her diamonds and pearls, just as I have put on a costume, my frayed cap and cape, and together our diverted souls walk the streets of Paris begging to find whatever it is that has gone missing.

It occurs to me that if I knock on your door you will either turn me away or take me in. I have nothing to lose for calling upon you. I turn the idea over, step away from the iron gate in fear, but then lower my eyes, and take hold of the latch. Without further hesitation, I throw it open.

I will love you, I promise. I feel it. My heart beats erratically as though Maman has stepped in front of me and warned me against this, for in her mind I am lost to finer things. I deserve my station. The wind rattles the gate and it swings away from me. These are unusual feelings. I know not if it is my nerves or if I am cold. I hide my parcel of mis-matched gloves in the shrubbery and smooth my skirt with my trembling hands. I tiptoe up the stone steps. It is beyond my dignity to turn. I must see you. I know of no other feeling, like this, at this moment. I am expecting the look on your face to be unpleasant, but I will explain who I am and why I am here.

The night air is getting sharp, the wind bitter. I have a grate to go to, but it is crowded. There are too many souls who come to Paris to scavenge about. And what is it that they hope to find? There are broken bottles, bits of soiled ticking, and a lost doll, but these are never enough. Yet they should be more than enough. Shouldn't they? How is it then that I want more? I continue to stumble up the steps and run a torn glove down my tear-stained face. I cannot deem Maman ir-responsible, I realize, just because she wanted diamonds. We want what we want.

I stand upon the stoop and turn the brass bell. It, too, is in need of polishing. All at once, you are frozen in time. I feel you belong to me and I touch the bell once more. I know not

how, but when your hand touched mine our lives entwined.
Are we not destined to encircle one another? The door opens
and you stand erect, your shoulders taut. There is unease. I
have interrupted your evening meal. I turn to look beyond
the vestibule but your house has neither columns nor a soar-
ing ceiling. You are alone. There is a fire. I take a step toward
you and you brush me away. I see that you have placed the
crushed roses in a slim porcelain vase, but the lonely buds
droop. The warm water has not yet revived them.

Did you know I stole those? Je les ai volé*, I want to say. I
needed a centime for something to eat. If you suspect that you
have brought home stolen goods will you throw them out or
will you continue to pry them open? Warm water should do
the trick and I think about asking you for a warm bath but it
is all too much, and just as you are about to close the door on
me I turn from you and run. I fly as fast as I can down the
slippery steps and through the swinging gate. Into the night I
dash, forever haunted by your touch.

*For translations of this French phrase and others, please turn
to page 203.

Two

Guy

I don't normally shy away from street urchins with such urgency, but there's something in your sorry eyes that frightens me. There's mischief, but there's also bewilderment and fear. I can think of a hundred reasons not to stop and engage with the likes of you, but I'm careful not to show this truth. I sidestep the truth. I won't reveal my fear, but if I get as close as I just let myself get to you, you'll pick my pockets clean. I'll turn and you'll pull away into the shadows then reemerge to steal. I can't afford to be stolen from. I don't know why I think this. Maybe I have enough. I certainly have more than you, but I can't, nor will I ever, engage in conversations I realize have no merit. And yet there is something about your azure eyes that moves me. You're not a child accustomed to restless nights, are you?

You're standing there bewildered by your lack. The centime is hardly worth much. I know it'll provide enough for tonight, but by tomorrow you'll stalk me and ask for more. I'll cross a different street to avoid you. I plan on this when my soft gloved hand touches yours. It is stiff with cold, ill-fitting, and the cracked leather is now hard and bent so I know not if your hand is really this shape or if you're hiding your delicate bones behind a mismatched pair of men's gloves. I determine you're not hiding a thing. You wear your desperate need upon your sleeve.

You have little in the way of manners. I can see that. The centime drops into an ugly riding glove and it dawns on me that you've never been riding. You don't know the pull of a carriage. Your soot-covered boots are anchored to the street. You can only lift them as high as a step. Should you ever find yourself in a carriage you'll not know to what speed the horse will trot. You'll become frightened. You'll shout. Your voice will be shrill, but I'll hold your hand and promise not to let you go.

I'm so stupid. I turn and walk away from you, alarmed at my desire. I quicken my pace. The flowers are wilted. I know they're stolen. I imagine you plucked them from a flower seller's rummage bin, or perhaps some lover tossed them into a vacant alley, along with her broken heart, and you scooped them up. I will throw them out as soon as I get home. I walk faster as the cold December wind turns in on itself. I dare to turn and look behind me, but you're gone, and as I step again onto the cobbled street, and cross where the lamp is brightest, I hear you cry. You will return to your grate. I fear you'll drop the centime before you can manage to secure a hot meal, but it's really none of my business what you do and how you get your soup. I have greater needs.

The wind sharpens just as I pull on the door. It catches. I struggle to secure my hand on the handle, and when I do, I see you again. You're across the street, the wind tearing apart your fraying cap, or what is left of it. Your body is nimble but strong. I can't tell if it's pride or defiance that lifts you upright, for you haven't a corset, but you stand before me without fear. What is your age? Sixteen? Seventeen? Eighteen? No, you're a child. I don't know what to do so I close the door and lock it.

Cook has lit the fire and prepared a light supper. She has built me a warm cocoon to come home to, but before she can leave for the evening I conclude I must close you out. I'll eat my supper with relative ease knowing I gave you the coin. In gratitude, I encourage you to go and find comfort for the evening, and I, along with my journals and my thoughts, will relax. I'll sit beside the new electric lamp and listen to the wind.

I like to listen to the stillness only to have it interrupted by discord. There's something about my disposition that recognizes false harmonies. I know the discordant chords and play them often. I have neither a wife nor a lover, for I have long ago missed out on my share of beauties. You will not be one. I don't attract what is beautiful.

————————

I'm aware that I came onto the pocked street at the exact moment you did, wilted flowers in hand. I turn this thought over in my mind. The fire is warm and there's a closeness to the room I don't normally feel now that I'm thinking about you. I toss back a whisky and throw a few branches onto the fire but they hiss and sputter. Stupid. I'm not thinking. The room fills up with smoke.

There are waifs much like you, wayward and alone. I see them every day. They rummage the finer streets disrupting what is pure. I hate to tell it like it is, but this is so. I can't help them all. Occasionally, I help some. I can't help them in the ways they need to be helped, but every once in a while I try. I always turn from them though, and in my haste to make sure I'm not further accosted, I pray they take my centime and use it to turn their lives around. What else can I do? There are others who do more. I do what I can.

I want to peer out of the drawn curtains to make sure you've gone but I don't dare. Did I do enough, I wonder? Yes. I will let you go. My supper is getting cold. I must return to what I know so I turn my back on you and take an ironstone bowl to the oak table. It is set with a paisley cloth and a silver knife and spoon. I say goodnight to Cook and send her home to dine with her own family. I don't need her at this hour. She ties her gray wool cape, the one I bought for her, around her shoulders and exits through the back door. I hear it shut. I'm alone. There's something steady in knowing that I will be alone for the evening, but within a heartbeat, there's something increasingly unsteady about it all. Is this loneliness? No. This isn't loneliness. It's nothing but feeling ill at ease and uncertain.

To tell the truth, I've not known love. I've tossed it around uneasily here and there, but only when I could stay away and never get too close. In my youth, I was probably loved by one or two girls whose hand I held but that was then. This is now. I'm six and thirty, too old for love.

———————

The fire hisses ungraciously as I settle down to a bowl of rabbit stew. I use this ladies' parlor in the winter, and take myself to the upstairs room in summer where I can open the large multi-paned windows and not draw in smells from the busy street. All in all, this is an acceptable, if not slightly pretentious, room in the winter just as the upstairs drawing room can be a very adequate one indeed. If I live an upside-down life it's because I'm often turned inside out and upside down. I don't always know the proper way. I like this overly decorated ladies' room in winter. For me, it's best.

The bell chimes just when I have let Cook go and I flinch, unaccustomed to the sharp sound. *Ç'est le plus désagréable,* I announce.

I look up from my supper in mock anticipation that my man will get the door, but I have neither the discretionary funds nor the stomach for a butler. I'm a simple man with few requirements. I haven't a maid. Cook takes care of the kitchen, the laundry, and the household duties. She darns my socks and rearranges the furniture so that I'm always warm in the winter and at ease in the summer. She toils, if toil is the right word, from sunup to sundown. I know she goes home to care for her own. I help where I can.

I send her presents at Christmastime (perhaps a new pair of gloves this year), and sweets for her children. I have made a nice life for myself. I shouldn't need a man to answer the door. I should never need. But in this instant, I need someone to address the interruption. I put down the silver spoon and throw the linen napkin onto my tufted chair. It's always best to lift oneself up with ease in situations such as this so as not to spoil one's appetite, but I catapult out of the chair and lunge for the door. I'm not expecting anyone. Who should be calling at this unfashionable hour?

———————

You're not a waif. You're beautiful. Stunning. Your crystal eyes shine through your tears and inflame my heart. They're strikingly clear and of good humor. You must smile often despite your wretched existence. I'm caught in a trap. I want to pick you up and cover you in kisses, but it's as though the shock of seeing you about to step inside my home negates all pleasures I feel. I step in front of you and sneer. Unintentionally. It's most unlike me, but you've followed me home and broken all rules of etiquette. But then I remember you haven't etiquette. You're a gypsy vagabond and I, your need.

Three

Emilie

I know that I have breached a divide I will never be able to repair. I never should have come to you. I will not set foot in this arrondissement again, and if I do, God is my witness, may you turn from me as you so want to do. I know your kind. You are heartless and cruel. You eat your supper and listen to nothing but your own false statements. The world is in need. I am in need. I was thrown away. I do not even know now whose responsibility it was. I never should have run away. I never should have been born to parents who took. I take. I ask. I need. Just as they did. Where will this train derail? And when it does will it bring me to my death?

I throw myself onto the grate and weep. I was wrong to think you would love me. I once loved my brother, but that was so long ago now I can hardly recall the sacrifices one must make to love another. I hold your centime in my trembling hand and chuck it through the grate. I don't want your money. I never want my path to again cross yours. There are abstractions far more important and this is not one of them. I cannot afford to lose. I will right myself. I will steady these tears. I will. I have myself to doubt just as I have myself to love.

Arrêtez! I shout when I can no longer bear the humiliation. Stand tall. There are greater needs than this.

———————

There is the mourning cry of a train whistle to contend with, but tonight I hear it differently. I hear not my parents' cry for help but my own. I imagine they died together in a mangled pile. There were bodies strewn, heads severed, corpses piled one on top of the other as I am piled onto the grate, one ravaged body next to another. There are mournful cries of hunger, but I will not be one of them. I turn away from the cries and thrust my hands into the mangled pile of dysentery. *Who stole my gloves?* I wail. There are bodies in motion, but they do not move toward me. *The lavender is my prized possession,* I shriek. Again, there is a stirring but no motion, as though the sea has brought with it a new wave, not unlike the wave before. It tosses aside what is new for the ordinary.

Maman and Papa once took us on a holiday to the sea. Henri and I clamored along the pebbled shore and stuck our toes into the waves. I can still taste the salt air on my tongue, and as I am reminded of the pleasures of this particular holiday, I, too, am reminded of the fear. Maman took voraciously to the sea. She wore a bathing costume and swam with ease. Papa begged her not to, but Maman tore through his insecurities and groomed the water as though for all her life she knew of no greater sensation than the sea.

I can still see her in my mind. She dances. I want to dance and shake some sense into these wandering souls who sit beside me, but I cannot. They are stuck in fear.

Abandon your fears, I want to shout, but they cannot hear me. There is no sense to make of a life that brings one to the sea and another to the street. I throw myself into the task of finding my parcel, but as I do I upset the evening's peace.

There's no damned parcel, the men shout.

Retourne te coucher, the women cry.

I cannot rest until I find my gloves. I turn and throw my hands to the night sky and ask God to please help me, but either He is busy answering the cries of others, or He has little time for a wretch whose shoes are soaked in the blood of eviscerated vermin.

I need my lavender, I wail.

Four

Guy

I'm touched by the irregularities of light the streetlamp makes upon your tousled hair. It is a tangled mess, but this golden hair is either a glorious attribute to add to your fair beauty, or it's a reminder that you haven't the ways and means to tame it. Should you put it under a proper hat will you become more beautiful? Or should you throw caution to the wind and take your cap off altogether and soar?

The night is cold, and the wind, fierce. I turn, ill at ease, for the bed is a reminder of all I own. I make up my mind to go back to the street where I first saw you and give you more. I can't sleep. I'll not belittle you, or disrespect your unfortunate circumstance by singling you out among all the others, but it's just that Providence has aligned my life with yours. I'm too close now not to touch your heart or offer you something in the way of comfort.

Rest assured, I whisper, *I know heartbreak.* But the night will not give way to morn. There is a dream, and in it, the train. It reminds me of irregularities. Of death. I push the pillow over my head, and in despair, cry. The train is a constant reminder of Maman and the way a heart stays famished. *I once was a child to know famine,* I continue, imagining you beside me. *I saw her jump in front of the train and had I not, in desperation, wrenched myself from her hand I would have found death too.*

Five

Emilie

I run my soiled fingers through my hair and, in despair, pull. If I shave it off now I will be free of the past, free of the gloves, free of the bundle, the parcel, the hope. But I cannot imagine going without my talisman and the hurt stings. The losses are compounding yet I refuse to cry. There are more than gloves to one's name, I realize, and these gloves are merely attachments that go beyond the things themselves. I have dignity and solidarity with my own cause. I will not compromise this for a pair of soiled gloves. However, the tattered scarf I carry them in has a close resemblance to the one my mother once wore. *Maman,* I try, calling out to her, *it has your scent.*

If coarseness was her scent, and I do believe it was, then, like her sister Élodie who wore the scent of greed, she wanted more. I know my aunt would have turned us out of the house the minute she took possession of it. How is it that I want more? Aunt Élodie, probably never realizing she would get it all, has gotten all there is. I will be the fool to go to my death knowing I could have had the silk parasols and lace gloves.

Arrêtez! I shout, unraveling at the sight of a man running, cockeyed, down the street. *You have my things.*

The vagabond does not have my things. He has his own things. I know that. His parcel is not as fine as mine. I chase him through the narrow winding streets, but this only makes my lungs burn. I throw my hands to my hips and give up. *Go,* I whisper painfully into the copper-lit cobblestones, *I have been wrong.*

I look up. This avenue is next to yours. Have I unintentionally run to you without realizing it? There is a faint light bouncing unsteadily over the tops of the blackened chimneys. It will soon be dawn. I can either turn from you again or step in closer. *My parcel,* I sing, remembering that it lies uneasily in your shrubbery. What god has brought me back to you, I wonder, looking at the golden orb of morn. My wretched god. My wretched heart. Stupid girl. My talisman is where I left it. But then I remember that I must never see you again.

I tiptoe stealthily across the street. Your house is shabby in the uneasy morning light. It is not as finely painted as ours once was and there is soot even you cannot sweep away. See, I want to shout, ugliness follows. I peer from behind the streetlamp. Your curtains are drawn. No light escapes. You are not yet awake, but that is because you have slept in peaceful slumber knowing that your centime brought me comfort on a frigid night. Well, you want to know something? Your centime brought me more misery than I have ever felt. The night was cold, the boots insufficient, and my memories came flooding back.

I once wore cambric drawers that did not chafe. I wore black cotton stockings and a crocheted knee-length wool petticoat, a slightly longer plain white cotton one, an even longer white ruffled one, a pink taffeta one, and finally, if Maman insisted, the extra flounced ankle-length white petticoat with eyelet embroidery and lace. My muff was mink. And that mink, I realize, was practical.

———————

Your gate is open. I must have left it so, but this was unintentional. Did you not hear it cry, in unhinged shrieks, this windy night? I look up and imagine your second-story bedroom. You will be in a mahogany bed with flannel curtains drawn around you, and there will be a damask-papered wall. It is a fine apartment, I want to tell you, despite the fact that you are not as fine as you pretend to be. You wear silk to console yourself and brighten your dreary day like a peacock, but I can see right through you. You spend your money flippantly, don't you?

I laugh. You are dressed as a dandy but living in this quartier. I am not so ashamed of myself now. You have your secrets. You parade your wealth on your sleeve, yet you come home to this. Well, I want to shout, I have wealth too. I reach for the parcel, and just as my hands clutch the fringed shawl, you open the door. I am not expecting you at this moment nor am I expecting to see you ever again.

I...I, I stammer.

You do not move but extend your hand, ever so slightly, as if to push me away. I turn and run. There is adrenaline coursing through me like the adrenaline that courses through the wildest, fastest animals on the Sahara. I cannot stop. I, too, have become a beast and I, too, have blood that drives me forward. My boots slap the stones. I throw my arms about, flailing without realizing how easily I flail, or how hungry I really am. I cannot stop crying. I have been found out.

––––––––––

It is the image of the hand I want. Yours, in mine. But I want what I cannot have. I clutch the bundle to my chest in anticipation that if I can spill its contents down the sewer, or fling it far into the Seine, I will let you go. A part of me has been close to you, I think. I slept, without really sleeping, next to you inside your rusting gate. But you waited all night for me, didn't you? And when I reached for my parcel, my fingers clenched, you pounced. Je te déteste.

Six

Guy

Traveling at the speed of a coal-fired locomotive, I spin on my heels to return to you. I can't help myself. I must see you. There are icicles and the sidewalk is covered in light snow. I tighten the silk scarf, button the long wool overcoat, and open the door prepared for a blast of cold upon my lungs. I expect nothing to dissuade me from my plan. I will find you. You're too slight to go far. You'll be sleeping upon a grate, and when you awake I'll take you in my arms and carry you home. There will be millimeters between us. Your breath will become my breath, and together we will make our way home through the slippery streets. I'll assure you that I'm strong enough to carry you, but you'll insist on walking. And I'll laugh and tell you that your independence is beguiling.

The blast of cold air is nothing but a reminder of the night you spent outside. I lift my eyes, and before me is the vision I'm too numb to recognize. You're bundled in some other rag. Did you steal another overcoat sometime in the night? And a wobbly pair of men's galoshes? I can hardly breathe, you come to me so unexpectedly. I open my arms in sudden surprise. Is it really you?

Halt, I shout. *Cease! Thief!* There is utter confusion. What are you stealing from my yard? I grab the handle, pull the door closed, and bolt down the steps. You're flailing, and the contents of your parcel spill into the street. What is this? I stop to pick up a child's lavender glove. It is in pristine condition and I thrust it into a pocket of my overcoat. There are other mittens of foreign yarn, but I can't stop and pick those up. Not for one minute must I take my eyes off you or let you escape. There are dirty shadows and the dusting of snow on the streets complicates my bearings. You shed the galoshes and gallop fiercely down unexpected alleyways. *Hey hey,* I shout. *I need to talk to you.*

I never imagined a waif able to outrun a man with legs twice as long. *Please,* I plead, looking heavenward at the graying laundry on a line, *I'm here to help.* In all my life I've never noticed silence such as this. The street is empty. There is a pallor to the day not unlike your gray overcoat, and I call again, but you're lost in all the grayness, camouflaged, just as I am ruby red, flushed with exertion. Have you come this way or did you take a different turn? There are tracks in the snow but they're not yours. *Damn!* I curse, *what a vision.* I want to chase you down but it's all too much. Go home, Guy, I tell

myself. Just go home. You're out of your mind. That waif is
out to steal your heart.

———————

The day ends in frustration. I'm cold and utterly nauseated.
I never imagined poverty on this scale. There are old waxed
parcels filled with decaying matter, sodden newspapers, dirty
muslin bags, broken wooden crates, discarded wagon wheels,
smashed trunks, rotting cabbage, broken buckets, and sag-
ging clotheslines. Scoundrels in fraying clothing steal. They
belittle and complain. They wail. *Fait moi tiens*, the women
shout. Rats scatter about in your upturned realm. There are
bodies lying askew on the grates, drunkards who claw at me,
sexual deviants who need me, and children who beg without
distrust. There are pregnant women, ragged and thin, who
look deep into my eyes and beg me to have mercy. Sloppi-
ness, eagerness, and unreliability are all piled on top of the
other in a slipshod way.

There are pieces of broken furniture, dangerous kerosene
fires, and flattened mittens, muddied and torn. I walk behind
tar-covered buildings, in front of raked buildings, and beside
burned buildings, and it's all the same. There's a whole town-
ship of vagrancy. I cover my mouth with a fragrant handkerchief, but it can't stop the stench. I sidestep oily puddles and
look behind pocked walls. I can't move without sounding an
alarm. I'm tugged at, whistled at, belittled, and booed. What
more can I do? I'll go home and light a fire. How can you
not return to me if you must live like this? I'll open the door

to you. That's a promise. I look to the falling snow and pray there's a God to hear my plea.

Come home, I whisper. *I will tear myself away from my journals, my textbooks, and my needs just so I may glimpse your golden hair once more.*

———————

I don't care how bitter the wind, how desperate the sleet, I'll walk the streets of Paris until I can make you whole again. But it's no use. You don't return. Weeks go by. The winter winds begin to quiet. Months pass. I return to the bank each day knowing that I am, for the first time in my life, without a reason. I haven't a purpose that amounts to anything of worth. I count coins. I pass each day counting what's not mine, but at the end of the week, the month, I'm no richer than I once was. In fact, I'm without. I lack.

Seven

Simone

The champagne is flat. I dislike it immensely. *Enlevez-le immédiatement,* I complain. I want to open another bottle, but the butler is missing. Where is he? *Babette,* I shout, *where is our man? Fetch him.* But there are gaps in the scenery. *Babette! Where are you?* Useless wench. *Why are you insubordinate with me? Bring him to me.*

The train car is running fast, too fast, but I want another glass of champagne. I shake off the cobwebs to clear my mind. *Babette! Where are you?* There are others who could open the bottle for me, but where are they? What time is it? *Emilie,* I call. No answer. In my rush, my need, I pass my ruby red fluted glass, but there is no one to pass it to. Is this a dream? *Emilie?! Où es-tu?*

The sidewalk is slippery. I am on a cart. I am sitting on brocade. I am being handed parcels. I am floating along without a care. Over and over the images turn as if they are pages in a book. *Emilie!* Such a vagrant child, I complain, always off in her own realm. *Mon chéri,* I call once more, *your maman is looking for you.*

Eight

Emilie

Maman, I cry. She comes to me in a dream and I force myself to wake. Where am I? The sun is bright. There is a glorious new dawn, the very essence of vibrancy and hope, and I run my hands down the unstarched sheets and turn on the makeshift bed. But it is soiled and smells of urine. Although there are new sights from my little window, and I am glad I found some comfort after all these months, the bed is ruined. I lift the rumpled blankets and stumble over the children. I cover my mouth, for their stench has become unbearable. I cannot shake the feeling that you are with me, Maman, but that I have left something behind.

Where is my lavender glove? I cry. *Mon gant est manquant!* I am at a loss without it. I think of you, yet I dream of her. It is as though I have awoken her, or you have awoken me, or my mother has awoken my greatest fear. This childish need.

Paris is in bloom. There are poppies. I love poppies just

as Maman did. *Go away,* I whisper to the tempered vision of Maman and her distorted self. But it is as though you have brought my mother out of death and I must look at her once more. I am of her realm, and she, of mine. I do not understand. Who has my lavender glove, that part of me I lost so long ago? There is nothing comfortable about seeing a vision of Maman this way. I find it all so unbearable. I do not want her. I have no need. I am fine. I have flowers to sell. I do not want you or need my mother's pride. I do not need the glove. I want something so much more.

Nine

Guy

Cook retires for the evening. I'm alone in my upstairs quarters where the air is clear but stifling. There are poppies. I bought them from a waif, but she was not you. They sit with little fanfare in the porcelain vase, and I remember the roses. If I were sentimental I'd remember them with fondness, but I'm afraid of sentimentality. I'm afraid of the unequivocal disruption to my simple life. I have promised myself that I will not need.

Perhaps I tossed the wilted roses out, or Cook did. Either way, the roses were tossed and I returned to taking my whisky just as I have always done, and no, I was not so moved to shape myself any differently than I had been shaped before. I wanted to do good by you, find you, and help you, but you made that task an impossible one. There are other wounded souls to help, but they don't stir me to do more than buy a flower or two. There's more to do, I realize. I could give more and sidestep less. Sometimes I return to the window in the hope of seeing you. I return less and less.

I turn on my polished heels and return to my desk where I've begun to think in terms of a character drama, one I could write to honor you. I imagine myself a playwright, a Balzac, and you, my muse. I turn the papers over, stab them with my ink-stained finger, and curse.

I have begun this god-awful excuse for writing, I hiss, *to do right.* But you're not here to hear me, and my writing is in vain. I tear up the pages and begin again. In my mind my play is brilliant. I manage to detail the slums with as much accuracy as I can remember. I write the story just as it happened. I buy the roses. You follow me home. I frighten you.

I scratch my steel nib pen across the page and return it, hastily, to the inkwell. My hands are stained with the woodsy scent of money. It's not my money, but the money of others I continue to count. And when I come home from the bank I sit down to my supper and compose the memory as best I can. There are shadows. How can I write a play when I know nothing about you?

———

Cook rolls up her muslin sleeves and paints the wicker chairs. I can recall as a young lad sitting in similar porcelain-colored chairs when I went to visit Maman's great aunt, Maude, or some such name, who put on airs. She did not flinch. Or cough. Her hand was on mine to remind me not to stir. I do believe Maude moved something inside of me that day so as to permanently upend me. After meeting this translucent woman, who sat and stared, bemused, I never resumed playing as a child should play. I soon found enjoyment in watching other boys run rough in the street, and like my aging aunt, I preferred to sit and observe that which moved around me. I found more pleasure in holding a book or a tambourine than catching a batter's ball.

I return to the playwriting, but it's a jumbled mess of nothing, for nothing has happened. I can't just make you up, my faerie sprite. You'll only become some figment of my imagination. I construct a play without words because I have said nothing to you, and you, in turn, have said nothing to me. Where in this universe are you that I should know your lost language?

———————

The days slip away, and when I return to playwriting it's all gone. I've said nothing and there's nothing more to do. It's a disappointment, to say the least. I stuff the pages into the desk drawer hoping that one day when I am gone, and the world needs to know you, a more clever man will open my pages and read about the gypsy vagabond. He'll write that you're kind but unhappy with your lot in life. I must leave a memory of you to make it easier for others to know your world.

Ten

Simone

Emilie! Vite, vite, I scream. There is a rush of air in my lungs and it feels as if something like coal dust has entered. *Where am I? Emilie?* My mind is clear, but my body feels unhinged. I call forcefully and you shout. There is something urgent in your voice just as there is something most urgent in mine. We are in a carriage. We are on a train. I am eating oysters. I am eating dirt. I need you to slow down. I need you to hurry. *Emilie? Le train a déraillé!*

Eleven

Emilie

I remember the day my parents died as clearly as I remember you. Any other day I would not count, but together these two days equal one as they have both become distortions of the worst kind. I remember your pocket watch. It was tarnished, as though it never occurred to you that you should polish it nightly. And I remember thinking, how careless of you. Do you not want the picture of yourself to be perfectly polished? Is this not your intention?

The dreams come now with more ardor. I hear Maman call out for me, and I want to go to her for there is fear in her voice, but she is long past this life and far away. She is not here. Or there. I know not where she is. Is she riding a train in perpetuity? *Maman,* I try reasoning with her, *go to sleep. There is nothing I can do for you.*

My shrunken skirt (the one I stole from some wretched child) is ripped, and I pretend that I don't care, but I do care. I care about the stupidest things now. Yet no amount of caring for a tangled life will bring you back. You are gone as she is gone. If only I had a needle and thread I could repair the skirt, but I am without a needle, without thread, without hope. The skirt continues to rip because, at eighteen years, I have begun to fill it out. I can no longer pretend I am a girl. I am taking on Maman's form. I haven't a corset or the proper petticoats. I would love a fine new suit. I frown and tie the skirt around my waist with a piece of butcher's string, but this, too, will fail and I will be in tatters once again.

———————

I could return to you. I don't know what good it would do though. You would just turn me out. But if you could see that I need a new suit and a pair of proper-fitting boots, could you not take pity on me and buy me something I need? I know I have more than some. You have more than me. Maman had the most.

———————

I sometimes think about marching up to your door and asking for something sweet, but I do not need a piece of cake or a taffeta petticoat. I can have stale bread as often as I want.

I simply take. But it is not the same, is it? I want a gift. Your love. I hide these feelings from you, but more than anything I hide them from myself, and as the feelings of neglect begin to accumulate, and the dreams materialize more and more, I fear Maman will come to me one day and take me with her. I cannot live this long on loss.

———————

My hand is burned and the skirt is ruined. I scorched the fraying cotton on an open flame while cooking a sausage for myself. *Maman,* I curse, *do not come for me before I have known love. Do not take this from me.* The skirt is beyond repair. I could steal another, but the thought of stealing, when there are so many other souls more desperate than me who steal, brings me back to you. I should go to you and beg.

I will tell you that I once had a nursemaid called Babette who tied up my curls with pink ribbons. She spoke kindly and paid attention to my idle thoughts, although at times she was stern, deliberate, and unaccustomed to children who dillydallied, as I was known to do. To please Maman, I let her dress me even though I was perfectly capable of doing it myself. The most difficult part of it all was buttoning the buttons. I do not think women should be allowed clothing that makes them dependent on another. Do you?

I wish you were here so I could ask you myself. I would tell you of all the childish ways I tried to undo Babette. I knew more than she did about the necessities of becoming a woman, for Maman gave me more instruction than anyone she ever hired. But it was Maman's self-righteous need to be the best at her station that gave rise to my childish anger. I hated her for taking me up that rung of the ladder when it was so much more fun to go barefoot in the park. Why did I have to wear boots that pinched when there were other children running free?

Oh, but I had a pony. Her name was Marie. She listed somewhat whenever I rode her. Is that not funny? It was as though one side of her felt the weight of my anger and the other side the lightness of my being. I must have dragged her down with all those starched petticoats. Shall I tell you about the riding costume? It was identical to Maman's. Golden, or ochre, I think, although I have forgotten the exact shade. Maman even took the leftover fabric scraps and made me a doll's riding costume to match so that we should dress alike. I rode sidesaddle, as did Maman, my jacket smartly clipped at my waist with a skirt that fell to my ankles so as to drape over little Marie in accordance with some dressmaker's specifications. I loved Maman. I despised her. Oh, how I remember her.

Maman did not love me the way I wanted her to love me. She always dressed the part of an attentive maman, but she formed opinions of me and decided what was best. I know, because I see her in my mind, and what I see is her deliberate attempt to corral my thoughts. Why could I not speak my mind? What prevented me from having my own knowledge? I could stand on a stool and narrate the Lord's Prayer in

Latin, and recite Shakespeare, his sonnets, and his prose. I knew the Greek alphabet. I was never without a ditty or a tune in my head for some after-dinner entertainment, as all well-bred girls are taught to sing, but do you know that the very best of me was never allowed to display my true talents? The very best of me was pushed aside from Papa's visitors and returned to the nursery where I was given a needle and thread and made to sew. It is no wonder I ran away. I ran from a life I did not wish to own.

I only wanted pen and paper so that I could write what my heart knew, but then I was never given the chance to share my heart. I was instructed to recite what someone else knew. Always. I could not tell Maman that I did not want her saints, all of whom she promised would shine their love on me. What an archaic idea. There were no heavenly bodies to sing me to sleep. *You, Maman,* I wince, *were supposed to sing me to sleep.*

———————

The hand is wounded, and the thought of slipping on a glove to protect it from further ruin appeals to me. I do not know why I cannot stop thinking about my eleven-year-old self. Did I not lose her long ago? No. I have lost only the child's glove. I have not lost my determination or my resolve. I gather my thoughts and run down the list of things I will say to you when I come to beg. One: I will curtsy. This is the way it is done and I have already determined it is crucial. Two: I will look into your downcast eyes until you meet my gaze, and when you see me, truly see me, I will hold my eyes on yours until you remember. You will look into my soul and remember that I knew you at some other point along the way, during some other life, some other existence. Three: I will share my thoughts and you will love my reckless ways.

They are here, I wail, clutching my breast. There will be a moment of recognition. You will frown, but I will burrow myself into your heart, the fascia tissue, the limbs.

My thoughts are simple. I haven't ideas that will help cure hopelessness. I do not know the best way to send the roiling stream of sewage away from these streets and not back up into it. I do not know how to barter for I have nothing to barter with. My ways are the epitome of something lost. I have only my love to give so shouldn't there be someone who will take this love? I think I loved Maman, but I did not know that then. She took and took and left me little room to understand.

Oh, Maman, I whisper, *I never knew love had so many threads, and so little opportunity to stitch it all in place.*

My hands tremble. I know the way to your door, and I use the time that it will take to get to you to brush my hair, but this coarse hand does not slide through tumbleweeds. My skirt has come undone again and I am in despair. I cannot go to you this way. I cannot. You will not see me. You will see what I am not, and not what I am. I will fall once more to a force I cannot control.

Twelve

Guy

The wind is sharp and the essence of summer is now long past. I think about you as a distant face, effervescent, but without clarity now that the sky is gray. You're a memory of gray, I think, taking the delicate lavender glove out of my coat pocket and placing it on my desk. Yet you shouldn't be held to such a memory. I imagine you're deeply absorbed in yourself, as all young girls are wont to be, but there's something uncharacteristically sympathetic about you. I turn away from the window and thrust the lavender glove into the drawer. I will leave without it this evening, I think, for I have carried you to and fro long enough. I must let you go.

My polished boots slap the cobblestones with little fanfare. I walk briskly. Is there anything more to agitate my mind, I reason, or has it all become an illusion? There are street urchins who cut across shadows, but when I turn onto Rue ___, where you're not expected, I relax. It's a magnificent evening full of promise. Ladies spin on their delicate satin heels and gawk at one another while extravagant gentlemen, who pay for their baubles and essentially create these women, notice the cut of their lace across fair-colored bosoms. I won't search for you where I know you won't be found.

———————

Beauty is in the eye of the beholder. Are these gentlemen more handsome than I, more worthy? I question this, taking stock of what's not mine. No, I laugh, distracted by their sense of nobility. I can be noble. I am noble. I will become nobler in time.

Thirteen

Emilie

The wound festers. The nights turn cold again and I cannot imagine I have erred to this degree. My plaid skirt is tattered, torn, and burned, and the lines are now distorted. I haven't a clean bandage. My heart is torn. My heart, my hand, and my skirt are ruined. *Babette,* I cry, searching heavenward, *did you die? Is that why you left me? Why must we all die? It is not fair. Il ñ'y a pas de plus grande perte que la mort. Je pense que je suis mort à tes côtés.*

I know I will overcome the illusion of this life and come out victorious as all good heroines do, but there is something about my growing list of needs that outpaces what I am capable of. There are women who take my bleeding hand and bandage it anew, and I nod. Actually, I begin to cry. There is no more lying. I am destitute. The lies I have told myself are piling up. The warm grate is of little comfort, for I once slept upon eiderdown. I cannot eat my soup with a silver spoon because I no longer own a silver spoon. I once thought I did. Did I not? I cannot remember. The pain is so intense.

Fourteen

Cook

I open the desk drawer, not to pry, but to look. The lavender glove is getting soiled by the oil from his hand. I watched him take it out of his coat pocket where he's carried it for months. I can't help but notice these things. I observe. I watch. I know the glove has meaning, but I can't imagine what he's gotten himself so attached to. The periodicals lay unopened. He writes. There are papers strewn about the desk. The top drawer is stuffed so full of paper I can't close it, but I put the glove back where I found it. It's not my way to pry. I'll just look. There are pages and pages of his scrawling hand. What is this declaration, I wonder? Are you, sir, in love?

There are secret realms. I know we share not just the

knowledge of these realms, but the longitude and the latitude of our desires. He must have a mistress, and she, a child. I notice the uncertainty of his hand as he swings the gate open and steps onto the street. The lamp illuminates his back and, with a clenched fist, he holds his top hat tight. Night after night it's the same. He goes out after supper, and his boots scrape the soiled stones until he comes back saddened by the shadows on the street.

Of course, I'm the fool, I laugh, pushing the drawer closed and running my fingers over the whisky stains. Concentric circles fold in on themselves. I button my gray wool cape, the one he so generously gave me, and grin. It's about time the poor clod got loved, I think, my mind now at ease.

Fifteen

Emilie

Nighttime is the worst part of the day. There are women who wail and push me aside for a place on the grate. I once was loved, or so I thought, but now that my hand is healing they want nothing more to do with me. I am an obstacle in their way. I take up room. *You have a warm coat,* they hiss. *Me, I have nothing... Je ñ'ai rien... You have your wits... Me, I am lost... Je suis perdu.*

You will only hurt yourself if you hurt me, I wail. *I am not without my needs. I cannot get warm in this cold rain. Look, my skirt is threadbare.*

I have been pushed aside because I carry the illusion of warmth, but there is nothing warm about me. I am cold, and the thought of sleeping on the street is becoming unimaginable. I gather my ineffectual parcel, my weakened talisman, and pull myself up onto my feet. I will walk, I reason, until I can find another grate, but the grates are full. There is a trash fire, but so, too, are there many desperate men who warm themselves by it. There is the bottle, but I cannot understand the illusion of warmth that comes from distilled spirits. *There are too many fools,* I cry, *who believe in spirits.*

Someone tosses their boots at me for they are too drunk to know that they will need them in the morning, but the boots are worn through and there is nothing left of them. The leather is pulled from the seams and the treads are bare. I am appalled. *You can toss those to someone more destitute than I,* I shout. I hold myself tall. I will run away from my desperation until I can no longer run. I will sit until I can no longer sit. And when I am no more a part of this world, I will beg Maman to scoop me up in her arms and carry me home. I am losing the fight.

———————

The rain continues, but I am only aware of it from a far-off place in my dreams where the patter on the roof is something of a pleasant sound. I lift my head to listen. The bed is warm or so I think. Is this another one of those illusions when one is chilled to the bone and on the verge of death? I run my chafed hands down the wool bedding. There is soot, but there is always soot. Maman has come and gone for the night. Her cries were not so loud this time, and I sigh uneasily. In my dream I saw her toss herself across the train, but why would she do this when she had a lapis-colored lake to view? Why was she not satisfied with the crystalline waters that she should turn her head and look the other way?

I listen to the insistent rain and think that should I ever have the opportunity to ride a train, I will turn my head to look upon the lake. But then again, if I can turn the other way to gaze upon the stately mountain pass, I would want to see that too. I am not sure if I am on a train to Switzerland or on my way to some other emerald land.

———————

The bed is soft. I open my eyes to the new day, and although the room is pocked here and there with a hazy light, there is nothing yet to see. It is all a scrim. There is an odor of charred wool and I imagine that I am alive, but I am not so sure. There is nothing of beauty outside my little window. I turn my head and notice that the wall before me is burned. I can just make out the dark shapes of twisted rafters on the ground. They are piled as bodies were piled, burned as bodies were burned, on a train that derailed returning from Switzerland.

Water drips from the ceiling and into my hand. I pull away, in fear, and open my mind's eye to the snow-capped mountain pass, but the distortion of this new reality exceeds the dream. I am in a wet and soiled place. There is nothing resembling Geneva here. I twist my thoughts ever-so-slightly to enter the train car with Maman and Papa, but I have not come along on this trip. I have been left behind with our disagreeable nanny who cares little about me and showers all her love on Henri. He cannot help it though. It is the way the roulette wheel turns. There are those you will want to love and there are those you cannot.

Sixteen

Cook

He's been lost to greater deeds than this, but when I'm told of his desire to clean up the streets of Paris and find meaning in his life, I question him. *Are you concerned for yourself?* I ask. *For your safety?*

No, he answers uneasily. *It's not so simple or as straight-forward as safety or concern. I'm concerned, naturally,* he stresses, *for those in need, but I fear we overlook a basic premise of their desires.*

I nod, hesitatingly, and push aside the pan of oyster dressing before inviting him to sit. He looks first at me, and then at the kitchen stool where he notices the black scuff marks on the white paint. He runs his hand over the raspberry stains and sits. He settles in, pushes up his sleeves, then takes the hen firmly but tenderly in his hands. It's a strange man who enters a kitchen.

I find I'm at a crossroads in life, he tries. *I fear that if I do nothing about it I'll go to my grave a pauper.*

I laugh and take the hen from him. *A pauper? You're a fine gentleman, sir.*

I'm a lonely man.

You don't fool me, I trill, pushing the dressing into the hen's cavity. *A fool in love you are,* I manage under my breath. *Un fou amoureux.*

Is it obvious? he asks.

Of course it is. You mope about then take off into the night. Bring her here. We are not so formal, you and I, as to dismiss love. Bring your lover here.

He is appalled and stands. *I haven't a lover.*

Non? You take off night after night as though you do.

I take off so that I may contemplate my life. There's nothing, he says turning to go. *Rien!*

Seventeen

Emilie

Maman, I whistle, unable to contain my excitement. *Oh, Maman. Where are you? There is whalebone and lace.* I turn on my bed and pull the damp bolts of fabric out from under me. Buried below the mildew is a roll of aubergine. *There is aubergine, Maman!* I shout. She is with me, I am certain. Either I am in her realm or the train has brought me into some ruined dressmaker's shop and deposited me into finery I have not seen since I was a child.

I close my eyes and I can still see my eleven-year-old self. My bonnet was trimmed in mink. There was a light snow falling. The dark bays toiled as they pulled the heavy sleigh over the rutted lawn. There were doves, and with unusual sentimentality, Maman laid a black-gloved hand across the box. The doves were not hers. They belonged to someone else and we were taking them to the estate of some great man, a nobleman. Papa strode about the country estate with pride.

Or was it defiance? I could not see his face, but his posture said it all. Now that I can see into the past, I wonder, had they reached the pinnacle of success? Had the roulette wheel paid out this much?

I remember the snowy day clearly, as if it was yesterday. It was Christmas. We were paying a visit to a great man who had become influential in Paris. A senator? A statesman? The details are unimportant, but I do believe his influence was important to my parents' well-being. There were secrets, I am sure, for I once heard Babette sneak words to Nanny in such a way that I now know was mysterious. Along with hushed voices, there were darting eyes, and I remember how Babette used to scurry away in fear whenever Papa was in the house. What was she doing in his private study when it was strictly forbidden? Was she looking inside his desk? Fumbling through his things? As a child I was unconcerned. Now I want to know. What was she stealing?

———————

Babette was a discoloration in my life, neither happy like citron nor dull like puce, but always a vision in black and white. She was stealthy when she needed to be, yet jovial, easy-going and unconcerned with what others might pay attention to, like the cut of a suit or the Persian carpets Maman needed beneath her.

Babette was my friend, I think, as I turn the aubergine cloth out onto a cutting table. There are holes where mice have scavenged, but I continue to unroll the cloth until I find a piece that is unharmed. If I cut this, I realize, and ruin it, I will not have another piece of aubergine. And it must be aubergine. I could choose turquoise, but turquoise is gaudy. I know Babette would choose turquoise, because Maman once said she was the kind of girl to choose what was less fine, so as much as Babette was my friend, Maman was right. It must be aubergine.

I dislodge a bolt of damp muslin from the bottom of the pile, upending the cavorting rats. They crawl over my wet boots and I suck in the air like I am drowning. I imagine the murky water filling my lungs. I cannot breathe. I despise rats. They are the epitome of the bottom rung. The very bottom. I have never made a ladies' suit for myself, and as I look around the forgotten room, I can just now make out the extent of the ruin. There is not much here to save. I cover the turquoise with a piece of fraying muslin to keep it clean just in case I change my mind, but if I practice on the inferior fabric no one will have to see the mistakes. I promise myself that I can pull this off. I have been offered something beyond my wildest dreams, and no one, not even I, can deny there is a spirit, such as one of Maman's saints, who must be looking out for me.

I have stumbled into a necessity. The charred wooden beams cross over one another, haphazardly, or tip into one another ready to fall. There is a forgotten light that streams across the room, diagonally, through the cracks in the rafters, and it occurs to me that I am shaped by these shadows as I am shaped by the light. The building has long ago been abandoned, and the windows are blackened with soot, but no one has come to claim or further burn its contents. After a morning of organizing, rearranging, and cleaning a pair of broad steel scissors, I return to my bed of ruined wool and lie down. I close my eyes and envision Maman's steady hands upon mine.

I need your help, I whisper.

There is fine muslin for a pattern, spools of dry thread, and ribbons. I turn a piece of imported lace over in my hands admiring the intricate edelweiss woven in a blissful serpentine pattern. Although the lace has been damaged by smoke, and there are too many threads missing, the symbolism of the lace does not escape me. I hesitate, remembering that Maman died on her way home from Geneva. Should I use the lace to honor her?

No! I shout, burying it at the bottom of a discarded pile of cloth. I refuse the lace on the grounds that it is too far gone, but I know this to be a lie. Maman died wearing lace and I want nothing to do with her sordid lying past.

Eighteen

Simone

My cold hand is in yours and I am now fractured. Broken. Mine is but a fractured existence. I cannot cut myself loose. I want what I want. I once wove your love into a whole, Emilie, but I fear you are cut from a different cloth, one I cannot understand. Do you not want what I want?

Come downstairs, love, and sit with me, I whisper, champagne distorting the images before me. *You cannot keep to yourself this way. Always so alone. It is unnatural.*

I reach for another glass, but it is tipped to its side. I reach for the table but it, too, is tipped. *Emilie,* I cry, *être comme un enfant normal. Être comme tout le monde. Je sais que tu seras en sécurité.* You don't answer. *Why are you tipping too? Darling,* I cry, *come rescue me.*

Nineteen

Cook

I fold the child's glove into his handkerchief, knowing full well that he's lying. I'll do what I can to stop his heart from bleeding. If he refuses to go to her then I'll bring his love to him. How dare he neglect what should be his duty? His heart is bending in some upturned way and he has neither the wits nor the courage to bring his lover and her daughter home.

She must be a wealthy woman, perhaps newly widowed, for the lavender glove is of utmost refinement. I envision her elevated social standing, having come by her money the old-fashioned way, and she will make sure her daughter is as impeccably dressed as she is. I know this to be the kind of fashionable woman who wears silk in the winter and layers of lace. Obviously, he's chosen the finest kind, but Monsieur is ashamed. Does he think he can't afford her? Or her daughter? He sits and broods day after day, but love does not know currency or social standing. It should not know imperfection. Love is.

Twenty

Guy

I clutch the handkerchief, bewildered that I should spend what I consider to be valuable time on trivialities. I made the decision to let the vagabond go and now Cook has brought her back. The cobblestones are wet and my boots slip. I've spent extra time getting dressed this morning for this is the day I've chosen to go to the bank manager and ask for more funds. I will spend whatever monies I consider extra on these wayward waifs. I don't care which of them receives my generosity. They all need help. There is nothing more to it. We should all contribute, and if we all contribute there will be but greater ease in this world.

I stumble over my own footsteps, knowing that I should contribute more to make sure some poor urchin's life is more comfortable. I must do what others can't.

The walk is bitter. I tug on my hat and pull it down over my eyes. I will mesmerize myself into thinking I'm doing good when what I'm doing is blocking not only the wind but you. Damn! How will I ever be able to see what is needed if I'm always covering my eyes from you? I lost. Are you satisfied? I lost you and in doing so, I lost sight of myself and my way of life. I lost sight of the trivialities that make up the better part of my day. I've lost myself. And all because of you.

———————

Do not be bitter, I hear you say. In my mind, you're pulled into my embrace and I hold you close. I did not buy a one-way ticket to this life, you chirp, laughing. I can get off this train. I can get off.

I throw myself against the disloyalties of this life and shout, *Où es-tu?* But there is nothing more to do. I've looked and looked for you. My heart bleeds. The world is too big and the problem is too immense. I can't stop your pain, nor anyone else's for that matter. I can't corral it. Who am I to beg God for a better station? Why should I have more? So that I could give more? This is the seat I bought.

———————

The air is fine this morning. Brisk. I tuck in my chin and return to stumbling. I won't ask for more funds. Enough of this, I think. I'm prone to melancholy and this is nothing but a passing mood. It'll pass and I'll be fine. I have better engagements. I have…, but then I turn and study the sunlight as it caresses the side of the imposing bank building. The limestone facade speaks in varying shades of splendor. There is gray and now this light. You are gray as you are the light.

I stop and look up at the equally imposing entrance, and before pulling open the heavy carved door, I withdraw my hand and turn away. This is a ruinous world. How can I enter day after day knowing that it's the money you need? I want nothing more to do with counting monies. I want the realm you live in to be gone. I want.

———————

It's unrealistic, Guy, I think, chastising myself. Don't be taken in by the waif. She's a street urchin. You have better prospects in this life than falling into a trap that says you must fix her.

I turn once more and enter the bank. The lobby is bustling with important men who sashay their way across the sleek marble floor. Theirs is a dance they know well, and the sound of money being made, the tune they love.

Twenty-One

Emilie

It is unrealistic to think I cannot help myself. After all, I am my maman's child. I cannot be helped by you. I tried. And failed. I will make my way into the street and use this leverage of a fine new costume to my advantage. I know about the costume. I know how it works. I have seen how women use it, how men use it, and I know more than you do. I know how trivial it all is, but this is the way we have designed ourselves.

You, in all your bargaining, will marvel at my fine cloth and you will bow to me. You will know to wait for me to enter a room before you so that I will walk in first and all eyes will turn, first to me, and then to you. I will walk on the inside and you on the outside. I will hold your arm and you will escort me across difficult terrain. I will not be capable of stepping anywhere, really, without needing you. Yet, I shudder, what law is written that tells a woman this is what she must do? I turn the muslin over and begin the arduous task of repairing my wounded self. My mind is on you and not on Maman. If I can copy my worn skirt, take it apart piece by piece, lay the pieces down one at a time, outline their shapes as best I can and enlarge them, then I will surely be able to build a better construct of myself and thus persuade you that I am your equal. But the skirt is far too burned and shapeless to use. I must draw a new pattern and discard the rose. It is useless.

The shortened day wanes. I am shivering, yet it is not from the cold. I am extremely nervous that I will not be the only squatter to come inside tonight. After all, what child would not want a castle such as this? There is nothing more important than a warm bed at night, but I will tell them that I found this first. I will stake my claim to the bed. I will fight off anyone who tries to take my aubergine. I will guard this new life I am making for myself with every inch of myself.

Maman, I whisper, *there are holes. I know these vagrancies. I have seen the holes in your temperament. I have seen them in mine. There is nothing left to do now but fill these holes. I must fill what you have left behind in me.*

———————

It is pitch black and the rats return. I hear them, sense them, and turn myself inside out trying to avoid them, but they are ruthless vermin. I cannot sleep. I pull the tattered wool bed I have made for myself up onto the ruined table, and it is better, but not by much. Rats can climb. I stand on the table and kill them with a piece of charred timber as they crawl over the aubergine, but it is useless. I cannot kill them all. I hold the aubergine close to my heart and sing, *Mon petit minou,* crooning helplessly, *come kill the bastards.*

———————

Come rescue me, I whisper painfully. I was wrong to leave you.

Twenty-Two

Simone

Emilie, I think of only you, but the sound of crying or breaking or beating or berating rises to such a level I can only stop mid-sentence and listen. Your father refuses me. What am I supposed to do now? Does he not know my heart? After all, we are varieties of the same senseless pear, are we not? Do not sneer, Emilie. Maman is broken. I am catapulted by the force of his anger and it sends me spinning. Why must your father refuse me? I want only to be comfortable in a grand estate in the countryside and appear...but there is shattered glass. Uncertainty.

I am a simple woman, Emilie. I want what I want, but it is not a matter of choice. There are candies and sugars and flowers and, oh, do not deny you want these too. The shirt-waist collar is tight at my throat. I cannot breathe. I need to unbutton it, but the pearl button slips round and round in my gloved fingers. Wretched kidskin. *Mes gants vont devenir la mort de moi,* I scream.

Twenty-Three

Emilie

At first light, I determine that the only way to succeed is to look beyond the vermin and begin the uphill climb to another rung. I peel back the muslin and lay my hands over the soft material. It is not as inferior as I first thought, rather it is quite delicate, finely woven, and silk-like. The day brings with it a new understanding. These materials are more exquisite than I first realized. The rats will upend me if I focus too much on them. I must overlook them, pretend I am in a beautiful shop, and pretend I am a worthy designer. Women will come from all over Paris to see me. I will be sought after! And I laugh at the thought.

I save the muslin, realizing that it will make a superior lining for my new suit. Perhaps I will even have enough left over to weigh down the hem. I rummage through the discard pile until I find a simple cotton fabric to use for my pattern. As much as I will need time to do this right, I do not have the luxury of time. I cannot live in these conditions. I will come down with dysentery, or some such horrid disease, so as much as I would like this costume to be of fine craftsmanship, I am more concerned with speed. I must dive in.

The pattern is designed. I do what I can, but I haven't the eye for what the suit should look like, having never worn one before. Rather, I design it to be as stunning as sidewalk couture, but without all the heavy trimmings or pretense. As I trace the newly made pattern on the aubergine with a piece of charred wood, I begin to recognize my innate ability to create this new self. I am good at this. I slow down and focus on the task. I have my mother's stitch. I refuse to draw comparisons to her, however, because doing so will put me on the same level as a woman I have yet to come to terms with, but the skill that it takes to upend her will be that much more pleasurable once I realize her worth. She was a beautiful woman. Not only did she clothe herself in the most avant-garde Parisian fashions, but she wore her couture with an ease that only those with a natural flamboyance have.

I remember Maman's costume, the multiple layers of silk, the delicate stitching, the glass beads, and the hand embroidery. Well, I think uneasily, I don't want to copy her. I will refuse to wear the knee-length corset and shape-enhancing bustle. These fixtures are only for those whose personalities are too weak or ineffectual to recreate themselves. I do not have enough fabric to make my suit exactly as it should be, but I feel that I do have the talent to make it better. The aubergine is putty in my hands. I mold it, shape it, and re-align it to suit me. There are covered buttons, but I put them along the side of the skirt where I can reach them. I make my buttonholes as easily as you have made up your mind to disregard me and turn away.

Écoute, I shout, *there are rats gnawing their way around me, but I am here because of you, and I am doing this for us.*

The rodents screech. The wheels on my train car go as fast as they can to get me out of here and back to you, but there is something immensely satisfying about creating this new suit. I feel I will hate to leave this forgotten shop. I tighten the floor-length skirt onto my body. I make it as tight as it will go, and as long as I can button the buttons I will tighten it even more. I cannot predict how masterful I will appear, but the very nature of this cloth lends itself to my form. There is just enough fabric for a matching jacket and a pair of tight-fitting gloves. I design a plain white pleated shirtwaist to resemble a man's, for I refuse to wear the bust-enhancing ruffles.

I go through the week with little food, and scavenge what I can, but what fool would leave such a paradise as this and be found out? As my suit takes shape, I can begin to feel the shift, and the desire to see you again heightens. I will go to you the proper way, knock on your simple carved door, ignore the broken glass, curtsy, and remind you that we have met before. You will not know me, but I will mention the roses. You will still not recall. I will show you my soiled boots.

———————

The suit is the epitome of high fashion. I cannot take credit for it though. I feel it is the work of Maman and her heavenly hands, for it is a costume made from necessity and not by my own invention. *Je serai éthéré*, I whisper. I listen for a response. Perhaps it is my mother's spirit, after all, telling me that she is beginning to understand her wayward sprite. *We cannot be bothered by the formality of the past*, she will admit. At last.

My costume is not like anything you will have seen before. It is simpler and less formidable than most ladies' suits I see today, and the jacket, well, let's just say I am not so good with the high stiff collar so I leave it off. Rather, I make a simple round neckline to show off my long slim neck. I construct one voluptuous petticoat out of black taffeta, the finest fabric I have ever seen, and as I have never been able to render myself complete without stockings, I find that I can create something suitable out of a black silk-like hosiery material. I stitch the stockings with love. I love the way they fit my legs, and I fasten them around my thighs with pieces of baling twine, but you will not yet know that what lies under is just as impeccable as what lies above. I have made myself desirable.

Twenty-Four

Guy

March is a difficult month in Paris. It's not yet spring, but no longer is it winter. It feels as though it will rain. There's a chill in the air as the clouds roll in, and the thunder rumbles much like a train rumbles when she is climbing a steep grade. I look down at my galoshes and think of you. Damn! What a corrupt place. I simply look down at my dry feet and think of you. This is most unfair. I have everything you do not have and more. I take my afternoon tea in one of the more desirable tea houses on the Avenue Montaigne, and as I ask for a sweet cake, I realize my galoshes are an unnecessary necessity. Without them, my boots would get wet, but surely, they are an excess I can do without.

I come here when I want refuge from you. I know you'll never enter my consciousness whilst I sit and stare out at a formidable street, so how is it that today, of all days, I'm thinking of you? My hand shakes at the thought of you. I crumble. The almond cake crumbles. The wheels in my heart spin the wreckage of unspoken desire. Honestly, I see you as this winged bird, flightless, grounded, needing to soar. What, then, does that make me?

Twenty-Five

Emilie

It is mid-afternoon. I have scrubbed myself clean, rinsed, dried myself off with a piece of flannel, and buttoned myself into the suit. I tie up my hair with black ribbons fashioned with silk orchids and ivory netting to resemble a hat, polish the cracked leather boots as best I can, and run my hands over my face to brighten my complexion. The gloves are my prize. They are what make the lack of a corset beguiling, for without the gloves I could not enter the scene.

As it is, I must be careful not to display the boots when I walk, but I cannot help myself. I want to run. If I enter the tea house and can get away with this costume, I know that when I find you this evening, you will fall for the ruse too. If I can pull off this coup d'état, disassemble the ladder, and eradicate the rungs, then I know you will be able to love me. Politicians will need me. Statesmen will want to know my secrets. I will, rightfully, know my place upon this earth. I smile knowing that I just might have the wherewithal to fool the very best of Paris.

———————

The tea house is crowded, and the windows are glazed in moisture. I notice that the mullions are perfectly painted and I stop to watch the scene. Those who raise and lower their porcelain cups without looking down have read the same rule book. This, I realize, is the epitome of Paris. Everyone is on their best behavior. I recognize the brightly lit room. It is a stage set and I, an actress willing to practice her lines, know this is the only way to gauge the effectiveness of my costume. I put a gloved hand on the door, open it, the bell jingles, and the door closes behind me. The tea house is warm and smells of lavender soap and fondant, like something from my other life, but I fear the humidity will make my ribbons fall. All at once, I am aghast as each and every one of the patrons looks up and watches me skip.

What a fool I must look, I realize, touching my bare throat. I know deep down inside I haven't a chance in hell of pulling this off without a proper hat. I fear it will rain. Although I have managed to find warm cover inside, I know you will not be here. I will be alone. How will I get my tea? I won't. I will simply wait out the rain and then make my way across Paris to the unfashionable side so that when you return this evening from your walk I will come to you and ask you to remember.

Twenty-Six

Simone

The broken window is nothing but a shard of spilled blood. There is a soft rain, more like a falling mist, and the blood and the rain and the mud are all smeared into these abstract patterns on the train car glass. *Emilie,* I cry, *there are cow feces in my hair.* I want to rip the buttons off the high-collared coat, but I haven't an arm. Before I help you straighten your tie, love, I just want to say one thing to Emilie. Just one thing.

The brevity of your desire is nothing, Emilie, I cry. Rien! You are just as much at fault for pretending. Stop reciting your stupid lines. This isn't a storybook. You aren't some hopeless waif. You are an Aubert. Listen. Babette has turned you against me. Stupid girl. Worthless maid. Criminal. Look at me, Emilie, there are sweets. There is blood. Go against your very nature and you go against me. Va contre moi et tu vas contre Dieu.

There are pigs. Why in god's name are there pigs? I have been on lesser trains than this where there were cattle and sheep outside the confines of a dining car, but why are they here in such close proximity? Your father is squeamish about bulls. *Darling, you will need a corset when you turn eighteen.* The champagne is flowing freely now. I am dripping in champagne. *Here is the situation, Emilie. Ecoutez-moi. I love you,* I continue, reaching out my hand to touch you. But the wheels that go round are no longer turning. I clutch red roses. Their petals are falling.

Twenty-Seven

Emilie

I take another step into the room, and just like that, all eyes in unison look up and then down my body. I have unwittingly unlocked a hidden chamber in each and every one of these patrons, and I return their smiles by walking taller. Some part of this scene pleases them. But why, then, if I do not need Paris to approve of me, do I still want? I want you, Maman, to witness my coming out. I do want. I want the comfort of knowing I will be loved.

I left your realm in aubergine and I will remerge in aubergine. Please, Maman, I beg, looking frantically around the room at the upturned eyes, help me. I do not want this realm, but neither do I want the other. Maman, I continue, slipping my hand over a piece of baling twine making sure it is still in place, this is nothing but an abstraction. Where can I go where I will be whole? Where I will be understood and accepted? There are men and women who put down their sweets just so they can stare. What have I done to deserve this life, Maman?

Twenty-Eight

Guy

I don't immediately notice the door, but I do notice the eyes in the mirror upon the door, and as they turn toward you, I follow. You are in the mirror. All eyes return to the mirror, the door, and to the cut of your cloth. It isn't easy to understand, because I don't recognize you, but they do. You are a vision of perfection. There are no better dressmakers in all of Paris who can create beauty such as this. There are muffled gasps. All eyes go up your person and then down. Ladies touch their cuffs. Yours are plain and not adorned with lace. Women turn toward one another and scrutinize their ostentatious hats. Men pull in their chins and return to their wives, obediently, but within a millisecond of awareness, these women realize they don't want what they have. They want what you have.

I stand unwittingly, as if some part of this scene is mine, and take your arm, for I'm closest to the door. Politely, I do nothing more than ask you to sit. I'm the envy of the room. And as you smile and accept, you don't think about me in any way other than I'm a gentleman dressed in my finest where the highbrow take their tea, where the air is sweet, where the floor is clean, and the wood, polished.

The room erupts into a kind of animated banter. You're seated. You tuck in your feet. Are those a pair of men's boots? I smile uncertainly and look into your tired eyes. I don't recognize you behind the veil, yet I know I know you. When the decibel level of a convivial tea house returns, and a chair scrapes across the wooden floor, all eyes turn to look at you, askew. No one shall be caught staring, but those whose primary reason for living is to gossip frown at their own insecurities. They're bewildered by you. They're besotted by you. And your headpiece, or should I say your lack of a hat, will become the most avant-garde fashion statement these men and women will ever see. Within moments women will be clamoring to identify your dressmaker, but women of your kind never reveal that secret. All good women know that a secret such as this is a weapon worth keeping close to their hearts.

Twenty-Nine

Emilie

I feel as though the train car has overturned and the bodies in motion suddenly tip. I feel the jolt. I am seated, but I am slipping somewhere through time. I do not recognize you behind your deep ruddy beard. Why have you corralled me so? When Maman and Papa returned from Geneva in a coroner's box I was overcome with grief. I turned to Babette, but she was not there. Why would she go and leave me? *Babette,* I whisper ferociously under my nervous breath, *Parisian couture is stunning. Why then, do I feel it was Maman's spirit who tempted me to make it my own?*

Babette was wrong to leave. If she had not left us, I would have stayed. Henri would have stayed. Like good children, we would have easily tucked away our grief and never cried. I have tucked you neatly away, Maman, but you are reemerging. My hands shake. There is a cup and saucer. When was the last time I drank from a cup and saucer? I will spill the tea. I cannot do this. I reach for the gloves, carefully push my hands to my lap, and as I was once taught to do, remove the gloves where no one will see. You're impressed, although I cannot help but think you will question my chafed fingers. You watch me and smile, eagerly, and it is at this very moment that I recognize your melancholy eyes. It is you! Why are you still trying to dig your way out dressed as you are in your peacock blue? And why, I want to ask, did you come to me in a tea house on the Avenue Montaigne in a gentleman's new suit much too expensive for your purse?

———————

Is that really you behind that fashionable new beard? I ask. You raise your dark lashes and lay a hand on the table as if to reach for mine, but I pull away and hold my own for it is scarred. *You are the gentleman who bought my red roses.* Again, you look at me and frown. *You live on ___. In an old brick building. The paint peels. There is a red room. I have seen your room, your worn steps, and your vestibule. I once had a vestibule...*

I turn when a boy slips a silver-tiered tray of petite sandwiches onto the white tablecloth. He looks at me, smiles, then turns to go. His hands shake. You shake your head, but I am so hungry I take one of the cream sandwiches, hold it in my trembling fingers, and cannot help but take a bite. I look around the well-lit theater and take another bite. And another. You cock your head, bewildered.

There are sweets. The cake is more delicate than anything I have ever tasted. I recognize the frame, the photograph, the scene. I am in a tea house with a man I am destined to love eating his small cakes. The cake is sweeter than I remember, and the taste is beyond Paris, beyond Geneva, beyond the moon, and out beyond the realms of nothing. I have been nothing. There is nothing more uncertain than death, yet with it comes a certainty, I now know. You are not gone from me. You are not gone.

No, you say astonished, *it's you? The gypsy waif? This is preposterous.*

I have broken an important rule. I know not to eat. More eyes appear to turn my way but I am famished and the cakes are beyond comparison. How is it that you are in my story? I reach for another. Again, you shake your head but you are not commenting on the cake or the fact that I am eating while the fashionable ladies are not. You are perplexed, as I knew you would be, but I wrap a piece of cake in a napkin hoping to persuade you that my manners are not gauche.

Non, you say, *s'il vous plaît manger le gâteau. Are you not ashamed of me? I did not mean to stare. But is it really you?* I hold the plate of sweets for you, but you slide a curious hand across the table and take hold of my fingers. You look into my palm. *I know you,* you whisper. *How can that be?*

I came here...not expecting you. I came because I wanted to...

Your suit is the envy of all, you say blushing. *It's so...what is the word...couture.*

I know.

You're that gypsy girl? Now in couture?

I am that woman.

You're not serious, you say, pulling away. *You? The waif? You're not trustworthy.*

I take a sip of bergamot tea and return the cup to its saucer without spilling a drop. I can play this part, I think. You continue to stare at me, bewildered. Agitated. Your mind turns over. You appear angry, but you cannot shout. The tea house is a prison. It is an oasis. The tea is bitter and I want to throw it all up, but I cover my mouth with the back of my hand. You look down your nose at me as I pull my trembling hands to my lap and return them to my gloves. I have made the finest pair of ladies' gloves. Can you not see that? Why then, can I not persuade you to believe I am who I say I am?

You're the gypsy waif I saw all those months ago? In truth? You raise your voice. *In stolen couture?* I stand and toss the napkin from my hand into the chair, for it is too much not to be believed. *You're deceiving me,* you sneer, scrutinizing the gloves.

You compose yourself, momentarily, when I show you the cracked boots. As you beg me to sit, the fleet of curious eyes turns toward me, but you turn from me to watch those eyes in the mirror. It takes a long time to explain myself, and over the span of time that it takes to tell you the truth, you continue to question. There are more eyes, but they are no longer clamoring to know which design house made my suit. They are uncomfortable with the young lovers' quarrel. I lift my skirt, ever-so-slightly higher, to show you the broken laces on my boots. You turn away and laugh. You laugh loudly, at what I know is an absurd sight. Imagine! Immediately, all the patrons in the room laugh too, relieved that the beautiful people who shed conventionality love brightly. Perhaps they are thinking that someday soon they will love brightly too.

Thirty

Guy

You're telling me that you, the daughter of Simone and Jon Aubert, spent seven days in a burned-out dressmaker's shop and made this? I ask, waving my hand at you, dismissing both you and your new suit. Impatiently, I toss my gloves from one hand to the other as you take your seat again and nod. *Non. You're the waif who deceives.* But you look at me imploring me to believe you. I want to believe you, but I can't. It's impossible. *You didn't live in that splendid house,* I respond, pointing in the general direction of the finest mansion in Paris on Rue___.

It is the one with two large swans carved on the front door, you explain. I continue to shake my head in disbelief, but you beg, *Please believe me.*

You want me to believe you once lived in that elegant mansion?

Yes.

And that your maman and papa were killed in a train car accident on their way home from Geneva?

Oui.

What was the date?

4 janvier 1896.

You want me to believe that you are the waif who sold me red roses? For a centime? I can't help myself and I laugh. *You're that girl? And you're sitting in one of the more fashionable tea houses in all of Paris in a costume you made?*

There were rats, you squeal. *I worked night and day. I found the aubergine at the bottom of a pile of...*

I dismiss you with a wave of my hand. *Enough. I've heard enough. Come,* I shout, taking your hand and pulling you to stand, *either you'll return the suit or you'll figure out a way to pay for it.*

Thirty-One

Emilie

Please, I say stumbling, *there are eyes...*

Under your breath you hiss, *You're a liar and a thief!*

Please, I beg, slipping out the door and onto the wet sidewalk. You cannot help but scrutinize the soiled boots and you raise a fist. I don't know if your anger exceeds even your own self-control or if your jaw sets rigidly every time you speak. I trip along behind you as you take my hand and pull me down the street. *Voulez-vous s'il vous plaît ouvrir votre parapluie pour protéger mon costume?* I ask.

We stop while you fumble with the umbrella. Perhaps you do not want to see a suit of this caliber ruined. *Where did you take this from?* you ask again. Disillusioned, I look at you, your back rigid against the wet sky, and question your train of thought. Why must you turn from me again and again? Can we not share an understanding? I know you. Can you not see the flame of recognition between us? Why, then, must it constantly darken? *I have asked you a simple question. Where did you take the couture from?*

I spit, *I took it from a dressmaker's shop.*

As I suspected. Which one?

The one I took it from.

Don't be smart with me. Which dressmaker are you going to return it to?

You purse your lips as though all that is right about the world rests there, and all that is wrong lies with me. I pull away from you and laugh indignantly. *There are saints more precious than all the world, but you are not one of them,* I hiss. I am getting soiled in the rain, but you pull me into you so that either I may hear your reverberating heart or you can protect the suit. I know not. The coarseness rises in my veins and I shout, *In all the world I have never known evil. I have known illogic, laziness, and thievery, but never have I known a soul to fight just for the sake of fighting. I fight for what I am. I fight for the truth. I am a fighter and I will fight. For me.*

Thirty-Two

Guy

You smell of charred wool, or roses, or something in-distinguishable, but it is the scent of something wild and unimaginable. You're here. I hold you and taste the wool because you're this close. There are passersby who gawk as we take up space on the sidewalk. *Hush,* I try. *Let's go quietly now. I'll escort you...*

No, you say, pushing me away. *I will escort you.*

We enter your grotto. There are roof rafters piled on top of support beams on top of charred bolts of cloth on top of cinders on top of vermin. We're in an inferno of wet heat. The place reeks of moisture, desolation, degradation, and disease. I cover my mouth with my hand, but you push me further inside. There are shouts. I know they're yours. You're a whirl of fire. In anger, you spit and spin.

There is wet cloth and remnants of cut wool. You point a pair of scissors at my heart and show me the hemstitching and the discarded lace. There is a pattern. I can't imagine it, but you have begun two more skirts. One is a sage plaid, and the other, a summer lemon silk. There are four white petticoats made from splendid voile, each in various stages of completion, cambric drawers, and various other ladies' underthings. I am aghast. I have nothing to say. I can't even manage an apology. There is nothing to do now but pull you back outside and bolt the door, but you're bewildered and quite alone, you say, weeping.

You reach for my hand, pull it to your cheek, and kiss it. Perhaps, you don't recognize yourself at this moment just as I don't recognize myself. There is an absence of sound. There is nothing to say. There are no words that will ever be enough. I take your hands in mine and we lie down on your woolen bed. I undress you. Our bodies need this. We want. But there are holes in the ceiling and soon we are covered in a fine wet mist.

Thirty-Three

Jon

It is tempting at this point in the journey to retreat. I do not particularly like Geneva, nor do I wish to return, but something is amiss. I admire Geneva, her vistas and stately boulevards, but I would never trade her for Paris. There will be avenues I might enjoy seeing again, but then again, there are avenues in Paris I will look forward to coming home to. Simone takes my hand, but I turn to the window and complain. She needs more, she says, but I tell her we have too much. The train car hurls her toward me as she continues to explain, but the train, and the wail, and the shrill of her voice complicate the scene.

There is an unprecedented strangeness to the whole of our view. I return to my cassoulet, but there is something unusual. The train car slides. Have we arrived at the station? Emilie, love, I think uneasily, you go round and round with yourself. Always at a loss. Is this what is happening to me?

I feel a loss I cannot explain. Where are we? I glance at my pocket watch. There are hands that move backward and hands that move forward. My wife puts a gloved hand in mine, urging me to flee. She is nothing but an abstraction in time, upturned and distorted. Suddenly, there is a fork in my eye. The train car tips on its side and careens down the mountain pass at an acute angle.

Emilie, I cry, grabbing onto the overturning dining table. *There are chocolates, love. I will bring home candies.*

Thirty-Four

Emilie

This is the part of the story where the lovers discover they are not lovers but bodies in motion upending one another. I know I have erred, but what is done is done. I have erred so many times there is no way to know what is an error and what belongs. I haven't a moral compass, and if ever I did have one, I lost it long ago. If I had kept my compass I would be sitting by a fire with my brother Henri, needlepoint in hand. We would have a terrier or a Great Dane. I have not decided which I would love more, but as you caress my thigh, I am beginning to recognize desire.

What's your name? you whisper.

Emilie.

Emilie. Stunning.

I tug playfully on your smart new beard. *I do not ever want to know yours.*

You laugh. *I'll tell you it's...*

No. You are the one to not be named, I announce, covering your mouth, playfully, with my hand.

But you push my hand away, annoyed. *Whatever does that mean?*

I want to know you for who you are and not for what you have become.

Emilie, you laugh painfully, *are you so errant that you wouldn't know I love you?*

No, I respond, *you love the idea of me.*

You pull away from me. *I'm insulted. I don't know what it is that draws me to you, but I'm drawn. I haven't a choice.* I laugh, knowing I feel the same way. You look at me, and in all seriousness ask, *Perhaps we met some other time? Some time long ago? I feel I know...*

Some other lifetime, I try. *Some other time.*

You nod easily. *I will love you and marry you and make you a proper wife.*

But I turn from you. *I do not want what is proper. I cannot be trapped like Maman...*

Your maman wasn't trapped. If you are who you say you are, then she was as fine a woman as there ever was. She loved her life. All of Paris loved her.

She despised herself.

Emilie! How gauche.

I turn to you and kiss you passionately. *This is all a ruse. I cannot love you.*

Of course you can. I feel your heart. I feel this. You are the one.

I will complicate...

No. I'll help.

I turn away again, unnerved, for the smell becomes unbearable and the rats insidious. *Who are you and what are you doing in this hellhole?* I cry.

I want to know your kind.

———

That alone is a definitive answer I should take as a warning. You are not a saint but a parasite unable to render your life complete without first making sure you tangle yourself up in mine. I stand. I contemplate leaving. I will be remembered as the one who needed you and I cannot accept that. I look out beyond the ruined rafters. For a moment I am blinded by my own need to prove you wrong. You talk, and I hear you, but I am not listening.

I hear *please...it's not like me...this world is hell...* and something else along the lines of *you'll need me.* Maybe I will need you. Maybe you are the last stop on this train and this is where I should get off. It is all so promising and wondrous and scary. But what if you need me? You continue and I hear you plead, *We're destined.* You are right, I think, taking your hand in mine. You are absolutely right.

I promise I will love you, I offer.

Thank you.

I do not want you to take care of me. I want, I say hesitating, *a way of life that you or I have not yet found.*

Thirty-Five

Guy

You don't want to know my name. Strange. I don't know what other nouveau thoughts you possess, or how to walk in your realm, but I feel I must accept this or I'll lose you. We dress quietly. Your hands are steady and you button yourself up without asking for my help. You button the skirt, the shirtwaist, the jacket, and the gloves. I take the garments you have begun, the fabrics and the patterns, carefully fold them up, and tuck them under my arm.

I know you could buy me new clothes, but I want these, you say carefully. *You are right to bring them with us. Thank you.*

I'm pleased you're pleased with me. *I want to see your maman's house. The one with the carved swans on the door and that stern cupola on top.* You turn and question me. *I want to see it for myself,* I explain. *With you. I want to feel what you feel when you walk up the stairs of your former life.*

I will feel nothing. Rien!

You'll feel the weight of your errors...

Stop! Enough, you say, grabbing the untamed cloth from me. *I will feel nothing. I want nothing.*

Then I'm wrong, I admit uneasily. *You'll not feel what I imagined you would feel. Perhaps we should excuse ourselves from ever discussing your old self.* I have ignited terror in you, and I backpedal, but you pounce.

You are testing me, you cry.

I'm asking too much of you. I was wrong and you've proven it so. You are who you say you are.

No, I am not who I say I am. I have no idea who I am.

The day is bright, and under a cloudless sky we make our way, silently, to my apartment. There are chestnuts smashed. They dirty the sidewalk. I interrupt the silence to ask you if you would prefer to ride in a carriage, but you say you're accustomed to walking and that you need this. *Before you put me in a trap I would prefer to walk one last time.*

A trap?

A carriage.

I bow slightly. *Yes, it's sometimes called a trap. I'll not put you in a trap, love.*

You turn on your heels and pick up the pace. *You will not put me in a trap, but I fear I will put myself in one.*

We make love and the bed is a temporary oasis from your wounds. I know that while in bed you're able to see me. There are moments when you delight in me, but within the span of an hour or so, the confusion returns. I ask you again if we can properly marry, but I fear the gypsy in you can never be extracted. I promise you the love of a good man, but you turn and look me squarely in the eye.

I do not know the love of a good man. I know the love of a frightened man, a man whose whole existence was to please another. Please tell me the difference. What is love? Is a good man one who takes care of me, or a man who lets me go?

I'm bewildered. I turn from you and stare into the peeling paper. The walls are suddenly dingy and gross, and although I have far more than you at this time in your life, I fear you'll outpace me. I'm no match for these concerns. *My name is...* I try.

Shh, you say uneasily. *I will let you love me. I will allow this. I am merely a fool.*

No, I'm the fool.

I feel the sense of propriety is compounded with an urgency to form opinions based on what we need one another to be and not what we are. You look at me as if expecting me to agree with you. *Let us try again. I will take you to my former house on Rue___ and we will knock on the door. I will ask the monsieur to please let me see my old rooms. I will take you to the secret drawer in the fireplace mantle and show you my hidden treasures. I will find myself with you in that drawer. You are buried alongside me.*

Thirty-Six

Jon

In Geneva, the livestock comes at us like bullets. We are turned inside out. I determine this is an infraction, but for the first time in my life, I feel nothing. It is as though someone, perhaps God himself, has turned off the switch, and as I lie my head upon my wife's lap, our blood makes cartwheels over the ceiling.

I hurl myself into my next life where the grass is green and more expansive than anything I have ever known. It is as though this mountaintop, which is usually covered in snow and ice, is transformed. It is not muddied in soot but becomes the most vibrant shade of green. Paris is rarely green. It is gray. Paris drinks up color and spits it out into its dark parlors where the people are elegant, refined, and in need of a fashionable palette. Or so they think. But in Geneva, the color explodes in all directions and I see myself in emerald the way my wife must see herself in ruby red.

———————

There is a motorcade. Yes, that is the word. A motorcade. A large black engine pulls the steel carriage. I sit upon a driverless trap, and the wheels turn, but there is nary a horse to carry my elaborate coffin. I turn and look behind me. There are other drivers in sleek carriages, and their wheels go around, but their horses are absent.

I cannot drive this contraption without a horse, I fear, clutching a steering device, but my hands are not hands and my horse has been transformed into a winged goddess. A silver sprite. She spreads her wings victoriously and pulls the motorcar so that I may follow. *These are wondrous things, the marvels of modern invention, Emilie,* I shout. *You are smart and mysterious. Look! There are electric lights, an advanced understanding of the sciences, of modern thought, and philosophy. And in this realm, the faerie sprite alights upon this motorcar and guides me home.*

Thirty-Seven

Emilie

Did you hear that? I whisper cautiously.

What is it, love? you ask, taking my face in your assured hands and kissing me.

I heard a voice.

I heard only your labored breath against my heart.

I saw the realm.

You pull me up from your chest where I had fallen asleep. *In your dreams?*

I heard Papa.

You are concerned for me, but you hold me and caress my golden hair. *Is he well?*

I open my eyes and look around the room. *I know not, but he spoke to me. His voice was clear. Panicked, maybe. I cannot remember what he said, but it was as though his voice entered this very room.* I turn to you and explain, *Maman and Papa died, you know.*

Yes.

They haunt me.

*Shh...*you say. *It's nothing to be frightened of. Your maman and papa are safe.*

How can you be so certain?

Of all the things I'm certain of, it's the passage of time and the trust...

Do you trust death? I ask uneasily. *How can you trust what we cannot know?*

We must have faith.

I do not trust my faith.

I do, you say, seeming to delight in your new role. You say you are stronger now that I have come to you, but I fear I have weakened. I lie in your arms absorbing the muffled sounds of a busy Paris street and fear Maman's desires have now become my own.

———————

What is it you are afraid of? Anything? I ask, pulling myself from your warm body to stand on the hard wooden floor. I slip on the petticoat and allow you to tie it for me. Eagerly, you hold me in your arms and...I don't know...practice being you, the you who wants to love. I lean back into your arms so that I can practice love too. I fear this is an illusion of love, just as there is an illusion of the illusion, going as far back as we can go to where we are willing to pretend we understand happiness.

You turn me around and look me in the eye. *You're making assumptions that I'm afraid of something.*

No. I know that we are all afraid of something, I say with confidence.

But I can't focus on the fear, Emilie, you say, pulling away. *If I focus on the fear I'll...*

Slip it under your fine carpets.

You don't understand and you dismiss me. *No.*

Yes, you will. Maman slipped her unhappiness under the Aubusson. I do not think she was willing to confront her own mind. Think about it, I explain, taking the ribbons from your hand and tightening the petticoat myself, *you are so composed that I have no doubt you hide your fear. As she did.*

You're furthering the argument I'm making that you're making assumptions. You never really knew your mother. You thought you knew her, but you were a child. And you don't really know me. You think you do but...

I pull on the aubergine skirt and button it. *How can one be happy sitting in a parlor day after day with only a needle and thread? Or a stack of literary journals?*

Perhaps you wouldn't be happy sitting in a parlor with a needle and thread, but without your maman's skill...her teaching...without the ability to think for yourself...

I reach down and pull the simple white shirtwaist up off the floor. *I do not want to hear it.*

You're skilled in something very fine, Emilie, you say, taking the shirtwaist from me and slipping it over my slender arms while admiring the stiff uniform pleats. *Very fine indeed.*

I take a step away from you and tighten the shirtwaist across my trembling body. *And you are making an assumption about Maman.*

You laugh, unashamed. *I'm merely addressing the phenomenon of the parlor.*

It is not funny, I wince, pulling on my suit coat and gloves.

Where are you going?

Out.

Without a parasol?

I tip my head to the window. The sun is bright. I haven't thought about a parasol in all these years, but the desire to own one again burns ferociously. *I do not need a parasol,* I lie.

You laugh again. *There's a fire in your eyes, love. Is this desire?* You kiss me tenderly on the mouth and push your tongue against my lips. *Let me buy you a parasol.*

There is a hunger for a new pair of boots, I confess. You scoop me up in your arms and promise me you will not get in the way of my desires. I let you hold me. *I do not understand this, Maman,* I whisper. *I want.*

————

This question of going out without a parasol is nothing more than you asking if I am leaving without you. I have wandered the streets of Paris alone without Maman or Nanny or Babette or Papa or you for all these years. It is not the parasol you want me to have.

Thirty-Eight

Simone

Dear Emilie, I write, *the land transverses unto itself. It pushes up against the mountain peaks and rolls down the other side with such a pitch that I cannot see where the mountains begin or end. Your papa and I love our emerald isle. We must be careful of our footing, but the walks are beautiful. I cannot say enough about Geneva. C'est magnifique. I will bring you here one day. Je t'aime ma petite princesse. Yours, etc... Maman.*

I fold the postcard in my hand until it is a perfect square then toss it to the wind. *Écoutez, Emilie, il y a des vagues et elles continuent indéfiniment.*

Thirty-Nine

Babette

I've been to the sea. In my mind, I can still see the school-girls who shake off their broad-rimmed hats and run across the rocky sands. I see you, Emilie. You were always a studious, intellectual child, yet like a tethered colt, anxious to flee. I remember the mornings I came to your room and you were already washed and dressed. You were too old for a nurse-maid and you didn't need me. Reams of your father's writing paper lay discarded on the floor by your desk where I'm sure you were eager to put your mind, and all you cram into it, down onto the paper.

I remember you fondly, Emilie, but it was so long ago. You were like a sister to me. I can still recall the razor-sharp look. The need to know. I remember the way you cast doubt upon yourself, although this margin of error was nothing unusual. All girls your age want.

Forty

Guy

You take my arm as we walk down stately boulevards. I can't help but notice the way you notice those who turn their eyes to look. The aubergine suit is immaculate, and your matching gloves and silk parasol are the envy of those we pass. There are moments when even I forget you're not wearing a corset. The pull of my heart is on your hips, and the desire to undress you is greater than any other feeling I've experienced. You've taken me out of my old habits, and as we nod to those we pass on this desirable street, I realize we're no longer taking right angles. We cross the street along the diagonal.

I wish to return the lavender glove to you, but I haven't the courage to give it up. I touch the pocket of my coat where

I've kept it all these months and contemplate returning it to you. You can't go home, I want to say. This is your home. I want to hold you close. I want.

————————

I ask if you would like to travel to Geneva for the summer. It's an innocent question, one I simply ask. I can afford it, I assure you, for I can liquidate some funds. My money will no longer be tied up and unavailable. The sidewalk is crowded and you're taking your steps diligently, but without thinking. We enter a park. You stop and watch the children march along the pebbled path, but complain that their nannies don't understand their need to run. I assure you that their nannies are behaving properly, but then you shout.

You should let the child run. My God, what is this world coming to if we cannot even let a child take off her boots and be free?

Please, I say, pulling you back to me, *it's none of your business.*

If I had been allowed freedom, I might not be in the mess I am in.

I look at you sideways. *You're not in a mess.*

I am in a mess.

Emilie, I complain, the tone of my voice shifting to a higher note, *if you think you're in a mess you're troubled. Seriously troubled. You have a fine suit, a parasol, a pair of fashionable boots...*

The best that money can buy.

I smile. *Indeed.*

You turn again to the children, touch the unfinished collar of your suit, and speak assuredly. *You cannot afford me.*

That's for me to decide.

We walk silently along the path. There are crocuses in bloom and we move, in unison, to pick one of the yellow buds. *I see that you've finished your other two skirts,* I chirp, picking the crocus and putting it smartly into the buttonhole of my overcoat. *And just in time for the summer season. How did you complete them so quickly?*

You pull up your own crocus, hotly, bulb and all. *I have nothing else to do.*

I help you sidestep a puddle on the pebbled path. There are more children, but they are shy and hold themselves close to their nanny. I imagine you were once a rambunctious child eager to pull away, and as you pull away from me you step right into the puddle and laugh.

I would like to take you to Geneva. We can take the train.

Non. I have had unsettling dreams of the mountain pass.

Your maman and papa are not there, but should we go, perhaps you will make peace with their deaths. You dance in the puddle in your new boots just to spite me. *Please, Emilie, there's nothing I want more than to help you.*

You toss the crocus aside and clap your hands together to loosen the dirt from your gloves. *Whatever for?*

Because you don't understand humanity.

You laugh painfully. *I think you are very tuned into your own desires.*

This stops me, and I consider you. *I...well...I'm no different from you, Emilie.* The children look at you. They pull on their nanny and complain. You lift your skirts and show them your fine wet boots, but they turn from you and continue down the path. *Please. Let's walk on. Please, Emilie.*

I will go to Geneva, you say suddenly, *but on one condition.*

What's that?

I want to go as your lover.

And not as my wife?

Non. I do not want the expectation. I desire the kind of love I know is true, the love I felt when I first saw you. I want that feeling to return.

I will love you, Emilie, I whisper, pulling your hips close to mine. *Please don't be frightened.*

I am not frightened, you assure me.

You asked me once what frightens me. I'll tell you. You, Emilie. You frighten me.

That is because I remind you of your maman.

My mother?! I complain. *You're nothing like my mother.*

Your mother took her own life. Are you afraid...

Non. I'll keep you safe.

Me? you ask. *You will keep me safe? Then you will keep me from experiencing the fullness of my life.*

I'll help you, I offer.

Help me do what? you hiss. *Stay out of trouble? Is that your idea of me? That I will bring you trouble, or worse, bring trouble upon myself? You are afraid I will take you down onto the tracks you so long ago turned from, aren't you? You cannot fool me. You belittle your mother if you cannot remember her in all her pain.*

Remember her for who she truly was and not the version you wish to believe existed.

Forty-One

Emilie

I have erred, I explain, stepping away from the mud puddle. I turn, apologetically, to you, and take your arm again. *I do not know when to talk and when to be quiet.*

I can't expect you to know manners.

I was raised with the kind of manners you would be appalled by. The expectations. The discipline.

You are all calculating and you cheer, *All good for a child.*

I tell the truth, and if that equals bad manners then I refuse to apologize.

You are quiet and when you speak there is anger in your voice, but it is far off. I cannot tell if you are being honest. *I should've helped my mother, but I was a spoiled child. I should've done more for her. If I had...*

She was not your responsibility, I remind you.

You turn your attention away from me and toward the

children. There are colored ribbons on a bonnet. They turn in the wind and you smile. *I'm not upset. I'll make peace with my past. I would have died that day had I tried to help. She would've pulled me with her and had I died you, love, would be walking the streets without a benefactor.*

I raise my eyebrows. *A benefactor? Surely, you are something else.*

Your words are clipped. *I'm not your husband.*

No, you are not.

You refuse to know me. You refuse my name, Emilie. Soon people will talk. You can't continue to come and go from my apartment this way.

I told you, I say, holding myself close, *you are more to me than a name. I do not like names for they lack imagination. I do not like arcane rules.* I smile easily. *Besides, this is Paris...*

You laugh, but it is not the laugh of someone who is convinced. *You're a wild child. A sprite. And because you can't claim your soul you can't claim me. My name is...*

Non. S'il vous plaît. Let this be my way, I beg. *This is the only way I can love you.*

Nonsense.

Perhaps a faerie sprite cannot reason, I trill. *Nor rationalize.*

Forty-Two

Cook

He pretends to be married, but of course, I know he's not. He knows I know. They're preparing to travel to Geneva. C'est une catastrophe, I fear. His investment in her is unnatural.

The curtains are drawn and I'm sent home, but I have more interest in her now than ever before. I'll admit her figure is beautiful, trim, and strong. She flashes her glittering eyes at him and the melancholy lifts momentarily, but like his need for whisky the melancholy returns when he realizes he must have more. I'll not capitalize on my employer's pain. I have greater needs. But I do have a curiosity that draws me to her. I recognize her spirit. She is like my eldest. *Non,* I laugh, *not Babette. Emilie est moins sensible.*

Forty-Three

Guy

Love, I whisper, stepping in from behind and putting my hands over your eyes to hide the surprise, *I've something for you. It was my grandmother's.* You squeal. I realize you're not accustomed to being approached from behind and you sense danger. That was not a squeal of delight, but one of horror. *I'm not going to harm you,* I explain apologizing. But you are as skittish as a young colt. *Love, I said I was sorry.*

Love. Love. Love. Must you always call me love? I'm tired of being called love.

But, lo... I explain, *I love you.*

I know you do, but you frightened me.

I'm sorry.

I have to be careful, you know.

I frown. *No. I don't know.*

I have sheltered myself for so long I hardly know the meaning of love. I am not used to this. Your arms. Your surprises.

I'm offering you something you desire.

Love?

Yes.

I no longer know what it is I desire.

Forty-Four

Emilie

We make love, and the feeling I recognize returns. I love the feeling of loving you and I love the love that you delight in. You take me into your arms, where there is sweetness. We are good this way. Our bodies fit. Here, we erase caution, and any competition we might have for one another is mitigated. You swoon at the curve of my hip, the softness of my breasts, the turn of my body as it fits easily within the crevices of your own. Here, we are happy and content, an admired body lying against an admiring man, and I count the minutes less.

You had a grandmother? I ask. *Why have you never mentioned her?*

I have a few of her things.

I squeal with delight. *What things?*

This was hers, you say, taking a black velvet jewelry box from your bedside table, opening it up, and offering me one of your grandmother's gems. *This is the surprise...*

It is ugly and I cannot hide my regret. *You are offering me your grandmother's cameo?*

Consider it a ring, you chirp, pulling me into you again, placing it in my hand, and kissing both my hand and your grandmother's ghost.

The cameo is large and I will be expected to wear it at my throat. I hesitate and turn it over. *Your grandmother gave you this?*

You laugh uneasily. *Someone gave it to me. I call her Grandmother, but I don't know who she was. One day this trunk arrived. I was a boy still, in school, and there it was.*

Now, this excites me. *You were given one of your relatives' trunks?!*

We were poor, you say hesitating. With your strong arms, I let you shift me from one hip to the other, where you pull my soft derrière closer into you. *I doubt she was a relative. But I'm not certain,* you say, seeming to remember your past.

You must have had the surprise of your life when you opened it up, I squeal, delighting in the idea of a mysterious trunk.

I was unconcerned, you explain, gently rocking yourself against me. *There was an odd assortment of things: a few books, a paisley cloth, this cameo, and the silver.*

Unconcerned?! How dare you, I wince, pulling away. *All this fun from a mysterious benefactor and you were unconcerned about it all? What else was in the trunk?*

Emilie, you complain, *I wish you would ask me about my love and not the trunk.*

I slide off the bed and stand before you, stone-faced, unsure of what to say. *Here,* I complain, returning the cameo, *I do not want it. I will never wear it. Especially if it is nothing special.*

I think the hair on the back of your neck stands up on end. *Without Grandmother I wouldn't be here,* you shout. *You wouldn't be here!*

It crosses my mind that you are angling me, and I hate angling, so I try a counter angle. *I cannot accept such a treasure,* I say, bowing before you. *I could feed an entire city block of homeless souls with the proceeds from this fine treasure.* You cough. I think you are listening. *There are too many children going hungry, and if I wear this I will be reminded of my good fortune and their hard luck. I cannot in good conscience...*

Good god, Emilie, I'm not offering your people my love. I'm offering it to you, you flinch, returning the cameo to my hand.

The cameo is probably plated, and I recognize immediately that it is something my gaudy aunt would wear. I regret taking it the minute I let your hand hold mine, but I know that if I do not accept it you will find more displeasure in me and throw me out. I have come too far to go back to the street, I realize. Or perhaps I have not gone far enough. Which is it? I stand before you unable to decide my fate. I do love you. From the moment I first saw you, I loved you as though all my life you had been waiting for me. And I, for you. I begin to cry. I am genuinely overwhelmed. You take me in your arms and hold me. I fall easily into love when you give me your body and I am returned once more to common sense.

The apartment is not grand but adequate, your bed linen inferior but warm now that you sleep next to me. Cook is humble and simple, but masterful at making cassoulet. She has potential. I rummage through the pros and cons as quickly as I can. Geneva will break me, I think, letting you pin the cameo on my collar, but there are worse things in life than scratchy bed linens that have not been imported from Milan.

Forty-Five

Guy

The ride to the station is tense. You don't want to go to Geneva, but you've promised me. You've made decisions that make you anxious, for beyond this realm lies an unknown. I feel you need this trip to help steer your soul toward forgiveness and acceptance, and once you begin the healing you'll become the woman I know you can become. Although the mere mention of this sets you astray.

I've tried over and over to appeal to you, but I've only managed to make things worse. I want to thank you for accepting my love, but I know if I say anything more on the subject you'll bristle. We're lovers, and when we make love there's an understanding even you are bewildered by, but when I speak you're besieged by my words. I can't do right when I look beyond the caress of your thigh. Est-ce l'amour? I want so much more.

Forty-Six

Emilie

You are quiet. Your mind traverses the landscape, and before we arrive at the station you lay a hand on my sleeve and promise me I will delight in Geneva. *How do you know?* I ask, bewildered. You assure me that you know my soul. You do? There are numerous carriages in the street and men shout. The train is the least of my worries. I do not need this, but what is it that I do need? I do not want to return to the streets, a vagabond, but for the life of me I cannot figure out why I do not want the new wide-brimmed hat, the silk parasol, the summer shoes.

There are poppies and I am reminded of my resourceful summers in Paris. I love poppies. They dot the gardens in an array of colors. The landscape is altered when poppies are in bloom. I am altered now that I am in bloom. I shift shape to accommodate you, but in doing so new burdens arise. The hat, with a dead stuffed parakeet sitting upon it, is gauche. It reminds me of my aunt. I stole myself away from her because she tore through her role with such disdain; I cannot wear this without thinking of her. I take it off. I will not wear one, I realize. Who says I have to wear a hat when I prefer ribbons?

I untie the yellow ribbons, tear them off with my teeth, tear off the ivory netting and the silk flowers, and toss the hat into the street. Immediately, it is scooped up. You turn when you sense the commotion behind us and that is when you see that my head is bare. My golden curls are loosely tied in a fashion that excites you when we are alone, and as we clop along methodically to the train station I fashion a new chapeau, one I like better.

Forty-Seven

Guy

There are sixty minutes in an hour and it only takes one of those minutes to pass for a person to truly recognize another. The new hat, tossed to the ground, tells me in one stroke of your disdain for me. As much as I would like to push you from the carriage, I won't. Rather, when we stop at the station, and others are clamoring to exit their carriages and enter the bustling building, I act the part of the loyal husband. You take my arm and I escort you to the platform, where I ask you to wait for me on one of the low wooden benches while I confirm our tickets. There is steam from the engine. Soot. I notice the way the ground heaves in anticipation, for there are many colorful slippers of fine construction waiting to board. I look down at them when I know I should look up, but if I continue to look down at your feet I will not feel so undone.

I contemplate leaving you. You're wrapped up in your

133

new chapeau of colorful ribbons, and you delight in those who stare. There is envy, yes, I'll give you that, but you have thrown away my love again. I can't go on. Why, if I were to ask, must you love yourself more than you love me? What about me distracts you from your objective? The slippers that turn in front of you linger, as do the eyes that stop and stare. I can't return my gaze to you but turn away on the recommendation of my broken heart. You're a gypsy vagabond through and through.

Forty-Eight

Emilie

I do not have a ticket. Or my belongings. I have a saffron parasol, a pair of ivory kidskin gloves that reach well beyond my forearms, a lemon-colored silk skirt and matching shirt-waist, four slim petticoats I fashioned out of the resurrected voile, a recreated hat made from some ribbons, a few silk flowers, a piece of ivory netting, and on my throat, Grand-mother's cameo. I put my hand to my throat. The cameo is still there where you pinned it. The summer suit is nouveau for I haven't a corset. I had convinced you that I could fashion the voile in such a way that the suit would not require one, and you agreed, belligerently, but you agreed because you knew that I was capable. You would have preferred that I wear something less avant-garde and more suitable for travel, but you hadn't a choice in the matter. I get to decide what I can and cannot wear.

I stand on the platform as the train is about to depart. I

cannot imagine what is keeping you. Have you gotten on the train thinking I am already there? But no, that is not like you. *Where are you?* I plead, running from one train car to the next. There is the last cry of the whistle. It is impulse, or it is foolery, or both, but as the train picks up speed, I hop onto the polished brass step and I am pulled from Paris.

Forty-Nine

Guy

Weeks go by and you don't return. There is bloodshed. If not in my heart, then from my torn nails where I must continually pick apart the reasons why I loved you. I feel as though I've lost. You've won. You've won your freedom, but my god, I've lost the energy you brought to the room. Yours was a difficult pace, but the context of it was delightful. I throw away the whisky. Too many people either begin again at this point in the story or take refuge in the bottle. I vow to do neither. I will show my resilience to pain just as I will mourn. I won't toss you out so easily nor will I fuel my weakness with more drink.

The unfinished manuscript sits unopened on my desk. I think about beginning again, but I'm tired of my story. I toss around the idea of burning what I've written, but if I burn it I'll lose what we had. And wasn't what we had important? I want to extract the best parts and maybe burn the parts

I don't like, but I must recognize this: the good is always accompanied by something difficult. Damn! Cook scrambles around me like a butterfly too impatient to land. I just need her to go away so I can think. She sautés veal chops and prepares a soufflé. There are things she does in the kitchen I know are technically difficult to do, but I'm not impressed. Why has she suddenly taken an elevated interest in my well-being?

Fifty

Tante Élodie

Enter the villainous aunt, the misunderstood sister, the daughter, the wife. I wear several hats, all of which I have designed myself. I thrust out my chin and throw open the curtains at dawn, but the child is not here. Her bed has not been slept in. *Tellement bizarre,* I say under my breath. *Emilie! Où es-tu? We have a funeral to go to. Emilie,* I complain, looking under the bed. *Emilie?!* There is suddenly a chill in the room, a rustling of the drapery, and I take in a sharp breath. *Simone? Est-ce vous?* I fear my sister's spirit wanders so I frantically close the heavy door behind me and exit the room.

The air in Simone's cumbersome large house is fraught with commotion. This is one of the finest homes in all of Paris with a staff of twelve, so there is no need for this much noise, but Henri is beside himself with uncertainty. He wails for his maman, and I take myself to his room. *Shh, mon enfant. Ta maman dort.* I know that my sister does not sleep soundly. There is fear. Uncertainty. He senses it. *Your maman is coming, child,* I assure him. Coming where? Going to? She is neither coming nor going but lying on a bed in an undertaker's parlor. I cannot right my thoughts. I should look for Emilie, but the confusion is compounded by Henri's cries. *Little one,* I whisper, rocking him uneasily, *don't pull on my diamond earrings. Ouch! That hurts.*

Fifty-One

Guy

Months later there's still no word from you. I've retraced your steps and looked on every possible grate. Your lemon silk will be easy to spot, I think, but what if you have discarded your summer suit or made a new one? No. I know that would be impossible. The dressmaker's shop has been razed. It's now an empty lot. There are vagabonds who sift through the rubble to reclaim stray buttons or a thimble, but you're not one of them. I walk when I want to drink. I can't think. I've gone over our last day together line by line, but you were the one to disregard love. I didn't do anything wrong. I simply decided I couldn't go on. I didn't leave you on the edge of a cliff and ask you to make your way home. I simply took leave of my senses for one brief moment. What you've done was catastrophic to yourself. And to me.

Work is a temporary distraction from this thought of losing you, but when I come home and sit by a fire, and the monotony of the day expires, I can't escape the silence. There are electric lights in the streets, a beacon to guide you back to me, but either you've lost yourself to something greater or you never really loved me. I conclude it's the latter. I pull out the manuscript and burn it. I empty the contents of the desk drawer and the papers spill to the floor. It's here, in the back of the drawer, where I find your lavender glove. *How did this get in here?* I wince. I hold it in the palm of my hand, turn it over, and marvel at its small size. I wrap the glove in my handkerchief and put it in the pocket of my coat. I don't know what I'll do with it, but for now, I conclude it's better to have it than not.

I turn the drawer over, knowing I've hidden Maman's last Christmas letter in a false panel. I slide a piece of veneer away from the bottom of the drawer and slip the letter, dated 25 décembre 1871, out of its thin envelope. The paper is worn where it has been folded and there are several pin-sized holes. I used to read it every Christmas morning, in remembrance of her, but I stopped doing that, oh, maybe fifteen years ago. I don't need to revisit her again. I burn the letter. I rifle through the remaining contents until I discover only what is necessary to keep. I don't know how I'll feel about the glove tomorrow. Tomorrow is another day.

———————

Cook attaches herself to my concerns. She makes mince pies and we distribute them to the destitute. We don't do enough, but we do something. She recognizes that I do this out of guilt, and she's right, but guilt drives us to do things we wouldn't normally do. I carry your glove with me. I show it to your people but no one has seen you or knows your whereabouts. It's as though you've vanished.

———————

Geneva, Cook whispers uneasily one day. *Do you think Emilie got on that train to Geneva?*

Non. Elle ñ'avait pas de billet de train.

Nonsense. She's quite capable of going the distance with or without a ticket. Have you thought about going to Geneva to look for her?

It's never crossed my mind that a woman with limited knowledge of trains, a fear of the mountain pass, and a fear of what she might find when she crossed into Geneva, would ever consider taking herself there. I look at Cook, stunned. *Geneva? Est-ce possible?*

Oui.

Non.

Her spirit has departed Paris. I feel it.

I don't believe it. Non. She wouldn't be able to get out of Paris without a ticket.

Cook laughs heartily. *Emilie could get herself out of a straightjacket if you put her in one.*

Fifty-Two

Tante Élodie

What fool goes to Switzerland in the snow and then dies? Mon dieu, quel cauchemar. *Simone,* I whisper fiercely, *the children are more than I can handle. Now what? Where do you want me to look for your slippery eel?* I tell her that the child has gone missing, without a trace, and cannot be found. The wind blows fiercely, and I half expect my sister's ghost to slip out from behind the drapery and answer me. I insist that Simone use her wandering spirit more wisely to find her daughter, but my sister is not here.

I call upon the police, the physician, and the undertaker. I call upon whomever I think can help. We postpone the funeral for another day while the decaying bodies lie in wait. There are protocols to adhere to, but Emilie has upended them all.

A week goes by. I open the door of the house on Rue ___ and shout up and down the street. I stay up at night only to fall asleep by a dying fire. I slip into bed without concern. I stay in bed while others search. Soon, I cannot be bothered. Henri needs me. And I have an important decision to make, one that will not suit my sister, I am certain, but we must have the funeral without Emilie. There are indictments against the vagrants who camp within our vicinity, but either they have done nothing wrong (the business of being homeless is not a crime, I am told), or the judge cannot find proof that Emilie was taken. I know she would not run away. She is a child. Someone stole her.

Several more weeks go by and I attach Simone's black diamond brooch to my red velvet cape. When I remember, I look for Emilie's aubergine in the sea of gray. It is a beautiful wool coat, and she wears it well. *Emilie,* I call, but as I wander the streets and look for her in the sunlight-dappled parks, I realize there is only so much I can do. There are too many shadows. I walk further. *What part of Paris is this?* I complain. I will be accosted, I realize, scrambling back to the comfort of my warm fire. I send others to look. My husband gives it a turn. There are search parties and we try, honestly, we do try. I promise we do.

Months go by and the house is sold. I continue to search, but the prospect of moving out to a fine country estate seems too nice an opportunity to pass up. Henri will do well to stay in Paris, I think. He must have a proper school and congruent teachers to help him become worthy of his good name.

He will find her, I reason. He will search for her as a good brother should. I am convinced that one day when the world turns itself right side up again Henri will find the little gypsy child. What more can I do?

Fifty-Three

Guy

It's not the season for Geneva. There will be snow. I remember your concerns about the mountain pass, but I assured you nothing could be simpler. The train will pass through, I promised you. Now I feel the need to be cautious. I don't expect difficulties en route, but the train car accident does loom large in my mind.

Geneva wasn't always a part of Switzerland, but there are often discrepancies drawn on a map, lines seemingly fought for and won. I think I'm fighting for you. I stumble about the train car and it occurs to me as I take my seat that you could have been in this very place and looked out upon this very scene. I run my hands over the red velvet bench, searching for a thread from your lemon silk. I search the entire compartment for a piece of you. For a forgotten glove.

Fifty-Four

Babette

It never occurred to me to take you with me, Emilie. And why would I? How could I? The thought of it is preposterous, but I can't shake it. Over and over I replay the scene, and each time I recount the moment I left, I set the stage a little differently. The props are in place. There's a porcelain water pitcher. I throw cold water on you. You scramble. We fight.

I am not going to Maman's funeral in black, you cry. I strike your face with the palm of my hand. Your eyes widen, but you ignore the pain. *C'est impossible! It must be Maman's favorite color,* you shout. *This frock is hideous. Please,* you beg, scrambling out of the way when I lift my chafed hand again. *Maman needs pink.*

For the life of me, I don't understand my anger. None of it belongs to me, but in haste, I tell you the way things will be. There will be nothing to negotiate. You'll wear the frock I choose. *In the morning when I come for you, you'll cooperate,* I shout. *You'll wear the black frock like the good girl your maman expects you to be.*

There are shadows in the room, a chill. I walk a fine line, I know that, but according to your aunt Élodie, this incident has crossed the line. I'm let go.

Emilie, I would never leave you, but I've been dismissed.

———————

I steal the very thing you need. I take my love, and my concern for you, and dismiss you at the very moment you need me to be true. I can't shake the thought that I'm your arch-enemy. And when we meet again on some precipice you'll slay me, you the knight, a Jeanne d'Arc, and I, the fire-breathing dragon.

Fifty-Five

Guy

I step off the train. The air is cold, fraught with uncertainty, and I wrap a silk scarf around my throat. This is
an unusual time to visit Geneva, I realize, but it's Christmas
and there are festivities. Safe and happy people ask for and
receive goodness as though they haven't a care in the world.
I scan the crowds. There's a vagrant who seeks. Her eyes
pierce mine, and I see her, but not as I once saw you. Shaking
the snow from my shoulders, I continue down the platform,
but it's impossible to ignore her. I return to the girl and drop
a few coins in her wash pail and extend a hand to her, but
she offers nothing in return. No smile nor nod of her head.
Nothing. I want to take the money back, but I walk on. She's
in need, I tell myself. As you are.

Carrying two leather cases, one for myself and one for
you, I realize I'm carrying the burden of my mistake. *I didn't
leave you,* I whisper, stepping pensively into a horse-drawn

carriage. There are silver bells on the leather bridle and they clatter noisily when the beast takes a jaunty step. *I merely sought to teach you a lesson.*

Fifty-Six

Babette

I have done worse, I'll admit, but the damage is like a splinter that festers. One false turn and the whole of your world, Emilie, abscesses and comes crumbling down. I'm never in a position to explain myself. Your aunt won't let me defend myself. She knows the score. Your mother has made sure of that. I'm angry, but this is not my fault. *You're a child,* I scream, *who needs proper restraint.* But I have been let go for getting in the way.

———

In my memory, the black frock lays upon the white coverlet like a ghost of Christmas past. You are, in my heart, a friend. You cannot be anything but a wandering sprite, aimless in your grief.

Fifty-Seven

Guy

Your realm opens up before me and it's nothing short of ethereal. The silver bells that ring all along the avenues with each passing carriage become joyous. Soft snow covers the hideous and makes all that is gray happy again. I pick up my pace and walk briskly. There's excitement knowing that you've left Paris for this. The cold is not as cold and the wet is not as wet. This is pure magic.

I scan the horizon, peer into alleyways, and walk amid puddles. Unspoiled chestnuts roasting on an iron grate take on new meaning when they are eaten in Geneva, where the chestnut is food for a faerie queen. I slide aimlessly here and there on slippery stones, and I'm happy I didn't discard the galoshes. I've never been this grateful for something so simple. The winter sun is bright. There are tremors in my heart. Excitement. You're here, I realize. You're where you belong.

———————

My room is damp and icicles hang on melting rafters, reminding me of what I've lost. Days without finding you turn into weeks. I feel your presence in a way I can't explain. The search will go on, I decide. Tu es où tu appartiens.

———————

The search will go on. You're where you belong.

———————

The search is long. How can you leave me this way? Damn! Je te déteste. And you want to know something? I hate Maman for leaving me too.

Fifty-Eight

Babette

Knowing I'm on the verge of discovering the truth, but unable to prove it, I run from Paris and all she represents. I hate Paris and her upside-down vagrancies, the right-side-up indecencies. I want to ask, was that really honest money, Mme. Aubert? The heart bleeds. There is blood on a train car. Blood on my hands. I dream of you, Emilie, but I can't rescue you. Your mother has spilled blood between us, and even in death, she wins.

––––––––

I look for you in the cathedral in Chartres. I uncover your spirit in the rafters where vagrancies of another realm have been left behind. *Sweet sister,* I whisper, my voice shattering, *come home.*

———

My spirit breaks. *Mesdames et messieurs de France,* I cry, swinging my anger toward God, *you let her go. Why? Because she tells the truth?* I fall to my knees in front of the Holy Spirit and wail. *I'm sorry, Emilie. I can't unearth you. Tell me, do you grieve or are you happy in some other realm?*

Fifty-Nine

M. Rivard, Le Coroner

Le défunt a subi de nombreuses lacérations et fractures rendant le corps non identifiable. Personne ñ'est venu la réclamer ou l'a signalée disparue. Elle sera envoyée à la tombe du pauvre. Respectueusement soumis, M. Rivard.

I wrap her up in a sheet and pray that her soul is taken skyward. There aren't angels in the heavens strong enough to transport these lost souls. I can't reproach their worn bodies or their errant ways. I don't know why they do what they do or why they distance themselves from hope.

Paris is crawling with lost souls and I pray to God they find their way home.

Sixty

Guy

I can no longer wander the streets of Geneva in the blind hope of finding you, nor expect you to answer my most pressing need. My mother took her own life and there's no changing that fact. She was but a blush upon this earth. You're nothing more than a winged creature to have passed my way, and as I must make peace with your absence, I must also make peace with hers.

I will shape-shift this battered realm of mine with you as my faerie guide. I've been spared the difficulties, but has this made my fate somewhat easier? I shrug my shoulders. I don't know. What is easier about my life? I take a step onto the train platform and contemplate the return to Paris where I will go home to my apartment, my comfortable bed, and a fine dinner. It's not fair, I realize, but this is my life. I took help when it was offered. You did not.

Sixty-One

Cook

I clean out the grate, and amid coal ash, I find half-burned papers and the vestiges of another time. He has emptied the desk drawer. There is a coroner's report, or what's left of a coroner's report. I can only read the part about the body being unidentifiable. When Guy returns from Geneva he continues to wander the streets looking for her. He says it's not Emilie he looks for, but the memory. He looks for her, I'm certain.

We continue to bake mince pies and he helps in the kitchen as never before. I teach him how to roll out pastry dough until he becomes very good at it, remembering to keep it moist but well-floured so that it won't stick. Together, we remember Emilie, but he begins to talk less about her now and more about his maman.

I remember the motion of being taken, he recalls. *I was whisked away when the train came to an abrupt halt at the station. The brakes wailed. There were these hands on me and I dropped my cap. Of that, I'm certain. I don't know who she was, but I suspect she took me from the scene so that I wouldn't witness my mother's death. There are more memories now. They are resurfacing.*

Go on, I say, encouraging him to continue.

There's nothing more. I was taken from the station, sent away to school sometime around the age of five or six, and somebody paid the bill. The end.

And after all these years you've never found your benefactor? I ask.

Non.

Did you inquire at the school?

Oui. Ils ont demandé l'anonymat.

And no one has a record of his, or possibly her, identity?

Not that I'm aware of. It remains a mystery.

I remove the pies from the oven with a piece of burned cloth. He looks at the cloth and then abruptly stands. *I'll buy you a new cloth. That one is charred.*

Sixty-Two

Emilie

I haven't a seat on the train so I turn toward the first-class dining car and mill about. In less than a minute, I am offered a plush chair. A gentleman orders champagne. We are jostled about as the train pulls away from the station and the champagne spills. I laugh. I tip back my head and notice the cut of his cloth. I have surprised even myself, for his is exquisite. I have fumbled long enough on nothing, I realize, desiring the fine dinner he offers. We eat prawns and drink wine. He orders rôti de bœuf et pomme de terre casserole. I drink more wine. I talk about Maman. He asks me why I am traveling unaccompanied. I stumble. I haven't an answer.

I haven't a seat or a traveling companion. I ask him if he would be so kind as to accompany me. I make up some long-winded tale about you. You were late. I looked for you. He nods uneasily. He watches me fumble with my gloves. *I lost the lavender one*, I explain.

He lifts his hand as if to say, *Enough*. And then I am left alone.

———————

I haven't a ticket, a seat, or a traveling companion. I order a coffee. The boy brings it to me and nods. I order a cake, and he brings it to me and nods again. I don't know the meaning of his coy nod, but I smile again when he returns to the table with a piece of cream-colored stationery. It is folded in half and then in half again. I am puzzled, but I open the letter. It is not signed but I know it is from him. He apologizes for the abrupt departure and explains that his wife awaits him in Geneva.

The boy asks if I would like a piece of stationery to respond. I nod. I write. *J'ai besoin d'aide. Je ñ'ai pas de billet.* I fold it in half.

Please take this to the gentleman in first class. The one who bought my dinner. The boy tips his jaunty cap and scurries out of sight. Within the span of a few minutes, he returns with another letter. It is signed M. ___. Unceremoniously, I turn the third-class ticket over in my hand and frown while the boy escorts me from the first-class dining car and back into the realm I am destined to know.

Sixty-Three

M.__

Azure, the color of her eyes, damson, the color of her wet lips. I carefully slide my hand over the desire I feel and hold myself in check. She eats heartily, unlike my wife whose appetite is squirrel-like. I want to devour the roast beef, but I know I shouldn't bite off more than I can chew. She turns toward me and rationalizes her experience. As impeccably dressed as she is, she is a vagabond. The worst kind. I leave her and curse the fool who brought her my way.

Isn't it obvious that I should know her? Intimately? After all, if the gods bring beauty to this fair earth, and bring men desire, one cannot upend the natural order of this realm. She is a cult-like sensation. Cult-like? I think about my choice of words.

———————

She hasn't a ticket. Of course, she hasn't a ticket or a centime to her name. I caress my desire and write her a short note. She has captured something in me I can't explain. It's not her devil-be-damned attitude. No, I have enough of that myself. I can't pinpoint exactly what it is I'll fawn over, but I will fawn. She beguiles me with her effervescence, her ease. And what a costume! My god, she wears couture with guts. *Damn!* I curse, *what a hothouse flower.*

Sixty-Four

Emilie

Geneva is awash in color. There are lush mountain vistas and an expansive emerald forest lit by a sun as brilliant as any I have ever seen. I am torn. I don't know whether to return to Paris or exit the train. I want to see Geneva. When will I ever return? Perhaps I should see what Maman and Papa once saw. I know this is why you left me. You were too ashamed of your own grief to witness mine. I am not ashamed of my grief. I have none. *I am simply a carefree spirit in dire need of a hotel bed,* I laugh, skipping down the train car's filigree steps and into the unknown.

Sixty-Five

Guy

I feel driven to clean up the streets of Paris, but then, where to put all the souls who have nowhere to go? I can't do this alone, I realize. You need to think about me and come home. Please. Help me. The world is broken. We're broken.

There are cracks in the sidewalk, and when I step over them I think about the numerous cracks in your person. No one runs away from what is good. I throw aside the feelings that burn and burrow deeper into guilt. I hand out blankets and return to the train station hoping you'll come back. I watch the trains come and go. I circle the platform. There are less ambitious desires than to resurrect a body that has tossed itself into the unknown.

Maman, I cry, kneeling and looking onto the sooty track where she was once killed and disfigured, *Papa couldn't help his tumors. He couldn't help his death. But you chose to give up. And you chose to give up on me. Why?!*

————————

My mother doesn't answer. You can't answer. There are too many unknowns that will never be answered. Are you alive? Promise me you choose life.

————————

The weeks bleed into months and the seasons turn. I tip my hat to waifs, look them directly in the eye, and ask them to identify their wounds, as you once asked of me.

Sixty-Six

Emilie

M. ___ is met at the station and taken away in a beautiful calèche. I am envious. I have never seen a more beautiful rendering of a fashionable man dressed in his summer linen and straw boater. I watch him go. Within moments the driver circles back around and M. ___ returns. I curtsy. The dappled horses snort in the heat and paw the ground. I turn and look behind me, but he smiles, extends a manicured hand, and helps me into his carriage. There are these moments when I wish it was you, but it is not. You chose to leave me. This is not your horse-drawn carriage. These are not your hands.

I cover my sly smile with my perspiration-stained glove as we ride down the more fashionable streets of Geneva. I cannot reminisce about what has or has not passed, what could have or should have been. Your soul was troubled and unable to reconcile the desire you felt with the obligations you were held hostage to. Seriously, could you not see yourself?

————————

How did you really think you were going to get to Geneva without a ticket or a chaperone? he asks. This catches me off guard. There are butterflies. They dance without care on purple echinacea.

Maman was simply wild about butterflies, I sing.

And she died. Here in Geneva? M. ___ asks.

I do not know.

But you've returned to claim...

She was sent home in a box. As was Papa.

I see, he says gravely. *And you've come to reconcile...*

Non. Je suis venu parce que je ñ'avais nulle part où aller.

You had nowhere else to go?

I had nowhere else to go.

You're a vagabond, and the street, he says, opening his arms exuberantly, *is your existence. You have everywhere to go.*

The street, I say, mocking him, *is dangerous.*

Yes, he coos, laying a hand on my thigh. *Be careful.*

Jésus Christ. C'est inacceptable, I cry. I want to jump from the moving carriage. *You have a wife. I have a husband.*

He feigns surprise. *Really?*

Yes. I thought he was on the train, but he wasn't. And now I have to find a hotel. I will go back tomorrow. Straight away. M. ___ raises his eyebrows in sheer excitement. *But I have been given the opportunity to see Geneva. Maman said she always wanted to bring me here, and I believe that she has. Has she not?*

I don't know, he purrs, *she's dead.*

Sixty-Seven

Babette

If I see you again someday on the street I hope I'll recognize you. For all my days I'll feel the shame of leaving you, Emilie, but what was I supposed to do? Your aunt turned on me at a time she should have asked for help. There's nothing more shameful than that, but she was grieving, and I know that now. I had to go far from Rue __ and the extravagant pony carriages, the new clothes, the tantrums, and those endless pots of chocolate. Day after day you were given whatever your little heart desired and it spoiled you. Tu étais un enfant gâté gâté. You were a spoiled spoiled child. Can you not see how you've ruined things for Henri? You should have stayed.

Emilie, I shout, *you were wrong to leave. I was wrong to leave. Your maman was wrong to leave. We are wronged as easily as we wrong others. Remember that.*

Sixty-Eight

Emilie

Days turn to weeks and M. ___ spoils me. He delights in keeping me as much as I enjoy being kept. It is easy to comprehend. I know how the game is played, the rules of engagement and so forth. He spends evenings with me but then goes home to his wife. I haven't a care in the world whether he stays or goes. I have what I need.

———

M. ___ returns. He returns, I want to shout, but you are gone. You cannot manage the simple task of returning.

———

Weeks turn into months, months into passing seasons, and the passing seasons into years. I am a toy, toyed with, toying coyly with him. I have a babe, and when M. ___ grows tired of her cries, he takes his cue and exits. I can do nothing to please him. I do not understand. Why am I suddenly nothing? What does this mean? I fell into a way of being that did not include you, I think bitterly, but I was safe. I was secure without you. I did not need you.

I stumble as he swiftly takes my arm and escorts me to the train station. I cannot yet fit back into my traveling suit, and when M. ___ takes my arm and pulls on me to hurry, the cream-colored suit rips. *Oh, Maman,* I cry, *I will return to Paris in need.* I carry the babe without pride, without him, without her, and without you. I am without.

He puts me on a train and I wonder what my life would have been like if I had stayed with you. We fought. You needed. I tore through you like one tears through brioche. I was so hungry I never knew that you were hungry too.

Maman, I whisper frantically, *I am frightened. Where am I going now?*

Sixty-Nine

Guy

I return to the train station, but I no longer look for you. I carry the valise and take a step forward for every backward step I imagine you take. I once loved you, you know that, but it was long ago. There are other fallacies I'm sure we would have realized. You, with your needs. I, without. I dump the contents of my life onto the street. Metaphorically speaking, this is the only way I can tell you what I'm feeling. I don't know you. I once thought I understood the brush of your hungry lips against mine. *I understood nothing,* I shout. *Rien!*

Seventy

Emilie

This will not be easy. We return with a trunk, much more than what I had before, and the porter carries it through the station with ease. I haven't a centime to my name, but I persuade him that you will pay the driver. We are helped onto a wagon. There are too many eyes on my fatherless child, the torn suit, the tears. I look out over the boulevard for you, but you are not here. The wheels turn. I turn and look behind me, but the train station has lost its promise of adventure. I will return to you in the manner in which I left. Destitute.

Seventy-One

Tante Élodie

Summer fades. The air is less placid, and I demand that the window be opened, but I am discouraged. I am told I will get a chill. There is an electric charge to the day that I need to seize. I do not understand how I feel her spirit, but I do. Emilie was a child when she ran away, I wince, courting this troubling thought as it enters my mind. A child.

Over and over the wind blows thoughts of death and they encircle the bed. I lay a frail hand on the white coverlet and remind myself that she was but a child. I was neglectful, I know. I dream of her, but the dreams are nothing I can make sense of. At times she comes to me as a doe. And other times as a stag. Her exuberant eyes stare into my soul and I feel the chill. *Open the window,* I manage, the breath raspy, the anger rising. *She needs me.* I fear death. I don't understand it. *Wait, death!* I whisper. *Wait for Emilie. She will come to see the error of her ways.*

Seventy-Two

Babette

The crusty old lady dies and I dress her bloated body in crimson. I was convinced that if I returned, Emilie, you would too, so I begged your aunt to take me back. I did all that I could to comfort her as she waited for you, Emilie. And, I promise, she did wait until she could no longer do so.

The elaborately carved box is heavy. The undertaker, along with three other stout men, lift it up onto their broad shoulders. They carry your aunt to the parlor where she'll lie in wait until she's buried in three days' time. She'll be buried with your mother's black diamond brooch, Emilie. I have no ill will. What's left of that I gave to God in Chartres. But I bury my head in my hands and weep.

I pull at a loose thread on my white apron as the tears fall.

Again. Maman consoles me when I can't be consoled. She asks me why I grieve for a life lived long. I explain that it's not my mistress's life I grieve for, but for the life of one little Emilie who has never been found.

Seventy-Three

Emilie

Your house is dark, the curtains drawn. I knock on the door, but there is an empty hollow sound. I knock again in disbelief. *This cannot be,* I say, turning to the driver and pleading with him to be patient. *Hello,* I cry. *Is anyone home?*

He throws my trunk onto the muddy street. It spills open and my objets de Genève scatter. I touch the cameo at my throat. *No,* I scream. *I am telling you the truth.* He curses me and shouts. The babe wails. I hold her in my arms, and as darkness prevails, we are emblazoned in a golden halo of electric light.

Seventy-Four

Cook

Emilie. In my mind's eye, I hold the delicate lavender glove in my plump fingers turning it over and marveling at its fine construction. He once told me that lavender gloves were exceptionally rare, expensive, and exclusive. I close my eyes to try to find her again, but the memory has faded. I'll never be able to hold her tiny hand again, I realize, the glove long gone, burned one day in a fit of rage. I turn the thought over. I recall the mince pies, the endless night walks, and the way he returned emptier than the day before.

We had an Emilie, I tell Babette, a vagrant who came to us from out of nowhere. She dropped in on us as a faerie sprite will come to collect the soul of another. I'm convinced she took his heart. Could she be the very same?

Non, says Babette bewildered, my Emilie was cautious. She would never run away. She was taken from me and lives in some other land far from vagrancy.

What tall tale do you deceive yourself with? I ask, concerned about my daughter's carelessness. *Our Emilie,* I suggest, *was your Emilie. She was ethereal. Delicate, yet fierce. You speak of Emilie as a wealthy child, sensible, and cautious, but she was a child of the faerie realm. The other.*

Maman, what has bewitched you to make you talk in tongues? she says frightened. *My Emilie would never wander the streets of Paris without first coming to find me.*

She found us. I'm certain.

Babette puts an unsteady hand to her throat and pauses. *Non,* she says frightened.

How do you think she was ever going to find you?

The estate was easy to find. She knew the way. She could have asked anyone and they would have directed her.

She wasn't looking for an estate.

Non. I disagree. You're deceiving yourself if you think this faerie sprite, as you call her, was Emilie. Emilie was restless, I'll admit, but never so restless as to leave when the going got tough.

Perhaps she lost...

Maman, non, Babette cries. *She's not lost.*

I fold my daughter up in my arms as she weeps. *It's not so simple now, is it? Tell yourself why you left her and you'll have your answer, love.*

———————

The sun sets on Babette's tears. She turns toward the

window in the hope that one day she will see Emilie once more. I can still recount the terror in his eyes when he sold the apartment and called for a wagon to haul away his things. *I will lose her,* he said, *for good.* Occasionally, he'll send a picture postcard or a Christmas letter. He writes and assures me that he doesn't wander the earth because he needs to know the gypsy spirit. He says he understands wandering. It suits him. There are places to go now, he says, where he has never been: Istanbul, Stockholm, and Madrid. *I don't need a house full of furnishings,* he writes without regret. *I'll explore what I have not yet found.*

Seventy-Five

Guy

For years you come to me in a recurring dream. You knock on my apartment door and I open it. You're dressed in black. You extend a black-gloved hand toward me and ask for the lavender. I feel the urge to pick you up, carry you inside, and make love to you. But the ash in the grate reminds me that we were simply a composition. Our love was merely a composite of who we were at the time we met, of all that we were capable of, and all that was. We could never be what we weren't.

You return again and again, and each time you come to the door I want to strip away the black, take you in my arms and make love to you. I haven't a glove to give you. I haven't anything you need. I close the door, but not all the way. Nothing is ever all one way or the other with you, Emilie, so I leave it ajar. As you would do for me.

Seventy-Six

Emilie

I rattle the doorknob and pound on the door, but it is bolted tight. Locked. You have gone. And without a forwarding address or any way of knowing how to find you again, I am at a loss. *I do not even know your name,* I cry. I fall to the step and weep. *Where are you?*

The evening chill begins to settle in around us. I look, again, through the windows into the darkened room. There is an explanation, I realize. There is always an explanation. No one just exits this abruptly. Not even in death. I hold my daughter to my breast and promise her a steady mind. *I will find help,* I whisper. She looks deep into my eyes, and all I can see is your need. I try shaking away the feelings of inadequacy, although I think this will be impossible to do.

I thrust myself at your door again and shout, *Maman, Papa, let me in!* But there is no answer. I turn the bell. *Auntie, please take pity. I have come too close to death and I have seen the other side. Please,* I wail, pounding my tiny lavender-bound hands on the swans, *I don't know myself. I have wronged. There is wrong in this world. There is so much wrong with this world.*

The way my life has come full circle is clear. The tears come hard and I rock the babe, assuring her that her maman has her best interests in mind. *We will look into the situation,* I tell her. *Something is amiss.* She does not sleep. I cover my face with my hands so she will not look deep into my soul. *You sold the house out from under me,* I shudder in disbelief. *You have deserted me for good.*

Seventy-Seven

M. Bourreau

It is impossible to see the appeal. My wife gives them money, but I refuse. I refuse them on principle. No one should stoop so low as to beg. No one. She is a beggar and a thief. I open the door expecting my daughter and her attractive family, but it is a harrowed waif. She looks up at me like she has just seen a ghost. Imagine, me a ghost. I am the image of respectability and ingenuity. I am a Bourreau. Listen. A Bourreau. I climbed my way up from a disadvantage and made a name for myself. I worked for this.

I work, I shout when she looks at me, bewildered. Her wretched eyes scan the expensive wallpaper and I cannot tell if she is looking for someone, or if she has come to steal. *Go away*, I hiss, closing the door on her.

She pushes on the wooden swans in a pair of stolen lavender gloves. *S'il vous plaît monsieur, où sont-ils partis?* she weeps.

Her hair is shorn and she is dressed in filth. *You are attracting flies,* I complain.

Pardon, she says bowing. *Ma famille? Où sont-elles? Où est ma tante? Henri? C'est ma maison. Où est tout le monde?*

Gypsy, go! I shout, trying my best to reason with her, but gypsies cannot be reasoned with. And that's a fact.

Maman, she cries, begging to be let in.

Your maman is not here.

Where is everyone?

You do not belong here.

Mais je fais. I do!

Non, I say abruptly.

I will prove it, she squeals. *There are sweets in the cupboard.* I push her away, but she continues to beg. *They are in the secret drawer. In the fireplace paneling,* she tries. *I hid one of Henri's tin soldiers, licorice sticks, a thimble...*

I close the door on her and bolt it. *Vagrant,* I shout. *Work for your sweets!*

Seventy-Eight

Emilie

I have no way of giving this child what you have given me, I realize, holding my daughter. I have no way of giving her hope.

The trunk is going to bind me to Geneva and all I once possessed so I leave it on the street and turn from you. Again. I haven't the words to explain it. Paris has wronged me. Geneva has wronged me. I will never be able to express the love I have for you, and you will never know me. I will walk away and we will never know what could have been.

Paris is gray. There are seeds of color here and there, but

usually, I am too hungry to look. My daughter beckons, as a child beckons, and I offer her my breast. I look for you, just as I look for Henri when handsome men pass the grate, but you are not here. Where are you?

———————

In my dreams, I feel your hand in mine, but when I awake I am reminded that the hand is not yours. It is my child's. In these dreams, you hold the lavender glove, as you would a child's hand, but I am no longer a child. That petite fille is gone.

Seventy-Nine

M. Bourreau

It is not until many years later, when my wife discovers the secret panel, that I remember the vagabond. My wife inadvertently pushes on the hidden drawer, and much to her surprise pulls out a small tin commandant. Alarmed, I push my wife aside. I rummage through the drawer and together we squeal when I pull out a thimble and floss, a darning needle, a piece of hardened taffy, and a picture postcard from Normandy. My wife puts the treasures on the polished table and innocently offers the tin soldier to our granddaughter, Lizette.

Non, I shout, grabbing my wife's hand. *These belong to Henri.*

Love, says my wife bewildered, *who is Henri?*

I look beyond the wallpaper, through the open door, and out onto the street. *Oh my god,* I wail, taking a step outside. *Oh, mon dieu!*

Love, what is it? my wife asks. *Whatever is the matter?*

The street is pocked with them. They rummage about here and there. I turn away and curse the god who brought her to me. *Almighty God,* I whisper, frantically taking my wife's hand and pulling it heavenward. *Put my vagabond back into the story where she belongs.*

Eighty

Emilie

Over the years the babe grows more beautiful. She has the eyes of a ne'er-do-well, but I have experience with her kind and know from whence she came. If she had my eyes I would understand her, but because she has his, I will give her the benefit of the doubt. She is a child of necessity. I have yet to give her a name, and I ask God's forgiveness for not doing so, but she cannot be named just as you cannot be named. I walk with her now, hand in hand, and we straddle a land that is nothing, as it is everything. We buy stale brioche and peddle flowers, never really knowing from one moment to the next just how we will manage, but we seem to do just fine. There is not too much we need. I once wore aubergine, and I teach my daughter the different shades and the nuance of color, but it all seems so far away and out of reach. I grieve for the time when I saw Paris in color.

I wonder though if it cannot be good, this gray. After

all, gray is the absence of white as it is the absence of black. I laugh. Or is it the abundance of white? The abundance of black? *Mon chéri,* I sing, turning to my daughter, *I think you are a Babette.* I lift her to the cloudy sky. I once knew a Babette. She was everything I should be, never afraid to love, never afraid of the truth. I should have trusted her. My daughter laughs and reaches for the sky, unaware of just how beautiful a gift she really is.

Eighty-One

Société Parisienne

We see the outline of her fine figure doubled over on the street when she is hungry, walking tall when she is fed. She is never just one thing. Beautiful, but in tatters. Rich in humor, but poor like so many. We glance at her askew, without ever really looking. We think we look and we think we share, but we are never enough for Emilie.

The cathedral bells toll, a reminder of all she is. She sits on the worn stone stoop, made even more worn by the number of steps we think she has taken to get here. She shows her handsome child the cornerstone of our society, once loved and trusted, and waves a delicately gloved hand to the sky indicating just how easily a flight of doves ascends. She hands out prayer cards, but we do not take them. We know the game and the way it is played. She wants our prayers, but for a price. We know it does not work like that, but she is not bitter. She dances and teaches her daughter the steps. We glance again, but they are gone, our faerie sprites unaccustomed to what was.

Eighty-Two

Henri

She calls her child Babette, and I turn. I once had a nurse-maid named Babette who stole a ring, a diamond brooch, or maybe it was an extra helping of cassoulet, a kiss. I do not know. She took something precious, I was told. A secret? In my mind, I think I see her, or I see the shadow of her. I see this child called Babette and it reminds me to look for Emilie. I have not looked today.

The gypsy child hands me a bouquet of pink roses, and I smile knowing these were probably stolen from some flower seller's rummage bin. Babette tips her head and extends a dirty gloved hand. I drop a centime into it before she clutches the coin and whispers, *Monsieur, if you offer the flowers a little warm water, the buds will open.*

I nod approvingly. *I will,* I assure her. She speaks elegantly for a vagabond. I study her soft round face for any concern, but there appears to be none. As I turn to go the sky opens, the rains come, and suddenly Paris is awash in a spring shower. I hand the petite fille my umbrella, but she shakes her head. *Non?* I ask. *You cannot be out here in the rain. You will ruin your frock.* Babette smiles and wraps her pale arms around her mother's neck. She touches her mother's cameo with her dirty gloves. The cameo seems strangely out of place, but nonetheless arresting, I think, on the slender neck of such a beautiful waif.

Babette kisses her mother's cheek and I hand the woman a fistful of francs. She looks bewildered for a moment as though the money is more than anything she has ever seen. I know it is more than she has ever known, but it feels good to be helpful. She takes the money. I see the wheels turn in her mind, and she looks at me inquisitively. It is not that she does not want it, but perhaps she thinks she should not get caught. I feel she is not accustomed to begging. I tell her I will return with more, but she shakes her head.

Please, no. This is more than anyone has ever given us. It is too much. I will...

If it can get you off of the street and someplace warm, then I know I will have done something good.

And this will make you will feel better? she asks, touching the cameo.

Yes. I will feel better.

The money will run out.

I frown. *Then you will need more.*

I will need more.

I do not know what else I can do.

Buy my flowers, sir, she says happily. *I have the prettiest flowers, the truest flowers in all of Paris.*

The truest, I admit. *You have the truest flowers in all of Paris.*

I turn away, although I cannot help but return. There is something compelling about them both, and I reach for Babette's hand and shake it. *Thank you,* I offer. She is suddenly shy and she hides behind her mother's skirts. I turn to the mother and thank her. She nods. I look deep into her smiling eyes. She grins. Imagine that? I linger, looking for sorrow, but she seems unbothered. Her flannel suit, and her daughter's pin-tuck frock, are impeccably designed. There is not a bust-enhancing ruffle in sight. Although of inferior gray cloth, their construction is avant-garde. Moderne. She slips the money into a secret pocket in her long slim skirt and tightens a gentleman's black alligator belt around her waist.

I step away again and sidestepping a puddle, return to my motorcar. I should inquire after her dressmaker. She makes wearing gray look so easy. My wife would admire her work, I think, but then I laugh out loud. The vagabond hasn't a dressmaker. That was not couture. I turn to look behind me, but the woman and her child are gone. I put my dark gloved hand on the seat beside me and pull the drooping roses to my heart. I usually throw away the flowers, knowing that I have done my duty and given a vagabond the coins she needs, but this evening I will put the roses in warm water and coax them back to life.

Eighty-Three

Emilie

It does not take long for the childhood memory to re-surface. Babette is not yet ten, but she is the spitting image of my brother. I saw it in her immediately, and as she grows, she grows to be as I remember him to be. Whereas I am petite in nature, Henri is tall yet short-sighted. Does he not recognize her? I know it is him the moment he puts the centime into my daughter's hand. I know it, but I do not know it. Do you know what I mean? It happens so quickly, and after all these years so unexpectedly.

I turn the idea over and flounder with the money. I do not want to count it in front of him. There is more than we will need. Before I know it though, he turns toward the motor-car, this abstraction of modern life, and he is gone. I pull Babette to her feet. Together we laugh at the thought that a fine gentleman has made her blush. I tease her, and just when she turns pink, flushed with excitement, I realize my mistake.

One moment my brother is here and then he is gone. I catch my skirts and turn to Babette.

Run, precious, run. She laughs and takes my cue. *Run as you have never run before.*

Are we going to the trains? she squeals in delight.

Our soiled boots slap the stones. *No, love,* I sing, *follow that motorcar.*

Eighty-Four

Henri

I turn the motorcar down Rue ___ and glide easily out of town with the winged goddess as my guide. I whistle happily knowing that I gave to a child in need. I clutch the wilting flowers, remembering the moment when my hand touched hers, and all at once, the memories come flooding back. It is in a photograph: the child's round face, her wide smile. I clutch the wheel of my car as it turns away from them. Her mother's gloves were soiled but finely made. Non, I think to myself, it cannot be. And I turn to look behind me. I whisper uneasily, *Emilie? Was that you?* Non. It must not be. I shake off the feeling. It was merely an illusion. The world has not yet righted itself. She was but a figment of my imagination, gone from my sight as a faerie flees.

Translations

Page 13 *Je les ai volé...*I stole them.

Page 18 *Ç'est le plus désagréable...*This is the most disagreeable.

Page 21 *Arrêtez...*Stop.

Page 22 *Retourne te coucher...*Go back to bed.

Page 28 *Je te déteste...*I hate you.

Page 31 *Fait moi tiens...*Make me yours.

Page 33 *Enlevez-le immédiatement...*Remove it immediately.

*Où es-tu...*Where are you?

Page 34 *Mon chéri...*Sweetheart.

Page 35 *Mon gant est manquant...*My glove is missing.

Page 40 *Vite, vite...*Hurry, hurry.

*Le train a déraillé...*The train derailed.

Page 49 *Il ñ'y a pas de plus grande perte que la mort. Je pense que je suis mort à tes côtés...* There is no greater loss than death. I think I died alongside you.

Page 53 *Je ñ'ai rien...*I have nothing.

*Je suis perdu...*I am lost.

Page 57 *Un fou amoureux...*A madman in love.

*Rien...*Nothing

Page 62 *Emilie...être comme un enfant normal. Être comme tout le monde. Je sais que tu seras en sécurité* Emilie...be like a normal child. Be like everyone else. I know you will be safe.

Page 66 ***Où es-tu?...***Where are you?

Page 70 ***Mon petit minou...***My little kitty.

Page 72 ***Mes gants vont devenir la mort de moi...***My gloves will become the death of me.

Page 75 ***Écoute...***Listen.

Page 76 ***Je serai éthéré...***I will be ethereal.

Page 81 ***Va contre moi et tu vas contre Dieu...***Go against me and you go against God.

Page 82 ***Ecoutez-moi...***Listen to me.

Page 89 ***Non...s'il vous plaît manger le gâteau...***No...please eat the cake.

Page 94 ***Voulez-vous s'il vous plaît ouvrir votre parapluie pour protéger mon costume?...***Will you please open your umbrella to protect my suit?

Page 114 ***C'est magnifique...***It is magnificent.

    Je t'aime ma petite princesse...I love you my little princess.

    Écoutez, Emilie, il y a des vagues et elles continuent indéfiniment...Listen, Emilie, there are waves and they go on forever.

Page 122 ***Non. S'il vous plaît...***No. Please.

Page 123 ***C'est une catastrophe...***It is a catastrophe.

    Emilie est moins sensible...Emilie is less sensible.

Page 130 ***Est-ce l'amour?...***Is this love?

Page 139 ***Tellement bizarre...***So weird.

    Où es-tu?...Where are you?

    Est-ce vous?...Is that you?

    Shh, mon enfant. Ta maman dort...Shh, my child. Your mom is sleeping.

Page 143 ***Non. Elle ñ'avait pas de billet de train...***No. She didn't have a train ticket.

    Est-ce possible?...Is it possible?

Page 144 ***Mon dieu, quel cauchemar...***My god, what a nightmare.

Page 154 ***Tu es où tu appartiens...***You are where you belong.

    Je te déteste...I hate you.

Page 156 ***Mesdames et messieurs de France...***Ladies and gentlemen of France.

Page 157 *Le défunt a subi de nombreuses lacérations et fractures rendant le corps non identifiable. Personne ñ'est venu la réclamer ou l'a signalée disparue. Elle sera envoyée à la tombe du pauvre. Respectueusement soumis, M. Rivard...*The deceased suffered numerous lacerations and fractures rendering the body unidentifiable. No one came to claim her or report her missing. She will be sent to the pauper's grave. Respectfully submitted, M. Rivard.

Page 160 *Oui. Ils ont demandé l'anonymat...*Yes. They requested anonymity.

Page 161 *Rôti de bœuf et pomme de terre casserole...*Roast beef and potato casserole.

Page 162 *J'ai besoin d'aide. Je ñ'ai pas de billet...*I need help. I don't have a ticket.

Page 169 *Non. Je suis venu parce que je ñ'avais nulle part où aller...*I came because I had nowhere to go.

Page 171 *Tu étais un enfant gâté gâté...*You were a spoiled spoiled child.

Page 189 *S'il vous plaît monsieur, où sont-ils partis?...*Please, sir, where did they go?

Page 187 *Pardon...Ma famille? Où sont-elles? Où est ma tante? Henri? C'est ma maison. Où est tout le monde?...*Excuse me My family? Where are they? Where is my aunt? Henri? This is my house. Where is everyone?

   *Mais je fais...*But I do.

Page 189 *Petite fille...*Little girl.

Author's Note

Restless, like *Room Service Please*, began as a novel, a somewhat long and wordy one. Rather than have it become a heavy-handed iteration of an early 1900s story, with lengthy descriptions and a lot of words, I decided to play with the format and create space for something new. By focusing on how I could write effectively with fewer words and still use each word to carry the weight of action, description, and character, I wanted to turn the idea of a "literary novel" inside out. Did I succeed? That's to be determined. By tossing extraneous words and using what was left more effectively, I realized that I was, in a way, crafting a prose poem.

I threw out all the preconceived notions I had about what this story should be and decided to let the writer's voice dictate just how we were going to do this. I had to trust this idea. It was not easy. I struggled, I fought the idea, and eventually, I threw much of the manuscript away. I gave up on *Restless*.

Time heals. It took over twelve years for me to have the courage to revisit this chopped-up manuscript, but once I settled into the words again, I was able to find the poetry. *Restless* had become a "language piece." But it still needed an arc, the necessary action to drive it forward from beginning to end. To create this arc, I realized that I would need a gimmick of some kind to keep the language center stage while still maintaining motion.

Language is tricky. We don't normally think of language as the driver in a story. We think of plot, character development, action, and reso- lution. We want stories to have a time and place. We want carefully constructed, recognizable tropes. Sometimes we accept re-worked tropes, and oftentimes many are, but we have fallen into accepting that stories are an either/or kind of thing. They are often about good/evil, love/loss, war/peace, famine/abundance, freedom/bondage, etc., but in truth, life is nuanced. We are not so easily defined in terms of black/ white. We create gray. I wanted *Restless* to represent that gray.

By crafting language to be front and center in *Restless,* I took the elements of a classic novel such as a Dickens or an Austin or a Brontë and shot it to bits. I didn't want my story to be just about love/loss or famine/abundance, or to take a reader over endless terrain. I wanted to pull in the lens, tighten the focus of the narrative to be about the language, and highlight the gray, or the nuance, of All That Is.

We can experience any number of contradicting events throughout our lives, where we are in abundance, freedom, peace, and love, to then suddenly, without warning, have this all change. We might fall ill, face a loss, or find ourselves in bankruptcy, for example, just when we least expect it. But if we only look at abundance as good and hunger as bad, we automatically divide our lives into harmonious (good) and tragic (bad). We separate the threads. We think good can only be good when it looks a certain way.

I'd like to offer the following observation: there is both good *and* bad in our lives at all times. Although we need polarity to be decisive, polarity is not a this or that, but rather a this *and* that. There is never one moment when we're not in some kind of contradiction, so rather than divide it up into a this or that moment and give these moments boundaries, I like to think about All That Is.

We are loved as much as we are disappointed by love. Yes, we have moments where we feel one way or the other, but because contradictions exist, I feel we need to balance these contradictions within ourselves rather than emotionally flip-flop each time we experience something good and then something bad. By saying, I am both lonely and I am content, simultaneously, because both exist, we eliminate the push/pull of polarity. By admitting we are fractions of All That Is, we put less focus on the contradiction within ourselves and more focus on equilibrium.

Restless is a story of contradictions. It is a story of loss and acceptance.

By highlighting the gray, and having it become as much a "character" as the jewel tones I use throughout the novella, I wanted to remind readers just how we think about color. Are we limiting the narrative by looking at the world as either black (evil) or white (goodness)? Our world is black *and* white. It is not one or the other, but a study in contradiction. Can we find beauty in the gray? Can there ever be balance?

I use the technique of multiple narrators to give the story movement, create visual interest on the page, and help propel the idea that we're never just one way or the other. We are multiple versions of one narrative depending on who sees us and how they see us. I chose not to shift the sound of the narration too dramatically from one character to another, because it's a small book and I didn't feel like there was enough room to establish many voices. Rather than give each person their own unique voice, I decided to give the book a collective voice broken into multiple threads.

All writers, to some degree, use gimmicks. These are just a few of mine. Maybe you can find a few more!

Acknowledgments

I want to wholeheartedly thank the teaching staff and my fellow students and friends at Naropa University for the opportunity to write, read, and explore poetic language. I didn't set out to become a poet. If anything, I found poetry exceedingly difficult to understand and I never considered studying it, let alone writing it. But life has a way of taking you on a train car ride to new adventures. Having arrived at Naropa, thinking that I would study only prose, I soon discovered that the core curriculum of the Master's program was in poetry. I now consider myself extremely lucky to have met some of the finest creative minds there who helped me tuck in my chin and tackle the work, and at the same time set me free to make my own discoveries. Having been given the freedom to explore my unique writer's voice, I am grateful to have met the people who encouraged, shared, and taught poetic writing.

Thank you, Dr. Dave Ferruolo, for putting me on that train.

My daughters, Sarah and Lydia, bring me immense joy. I am forever grateful that you are in my life and shower me with unconditional love. You are both exceptional teachers. I love you.

Thank you, Winslow McCagg, for sharing your beautifully descriptive, yet largely unexplored writing style. By accepting the use of color as "character," I found a new way to harness emotion. Without understanding color theory and the complex interplay between the various shades, and their evocative moods and meaning, I could not have written this novella. I honor your artistry.

To Sheila St. Hilaire, thank you for sharing your divine inspiration. No one knows, because I haven't said one word in the manuscript or in the Author's Note about it, but I caught a winged goddess somewhere

211

in this work, and by doing so, tucked Mary Magdalene into the heart of the story. For you.

In gratitude to Sandra Bouquet Carslick for sharing yourself and your healing wisdom with me. I'm listening!

Thank you, Mom, Dad, and my brother, Chris, for your continued love and support. To Richard, Aunt Carolyn, Claire, and Melanie, thank you.

To Julia Connell, thank you for your discerning suggestions and for your continued support.

Thank you, Emily Kallick at Wildember Marketing, for the wondrously elegant cover design. Your illustration evokes the mood and artistry of an antique book—just what I was searching for. I am grateful for all that you brought to the design and for your continued help and support in getting my books designed and ready to print. Without you, I would be half an author.

To Lee Bumsted, thank you, once again, for your exceptional, never-tiring editing eye. This was a tricky story to write, much less edit, and I thank you for respecting the choices I made.

To Anna Thomson, thank you for the thought-provoking book club questions.

To artists, writers, and creatives far and wide, thank you for sharing yourselves.

Book Club Questions

1. The title of this book is *Restless*. Describe how and why the characters in this story are restless.

2. The author presents this story through "thought sharing" in addition to direct dialogue. How does this indirect writing style affect the story?

3. Emilie is a self-determined young woman who deals with her circumstances in unexpected ways. Describe her character and how it affects her decisions. What do you think of her decisions? Would you behave differently?

4. There are a number of objects in this story that have significance for the characters. Name a few of the objects and how they affect the characters.

5. Emilie spent several years in Geneva with a married man with whom she had a daughter. Why is Emilie silent during this period?

6. What is it about Emilie's character that leads her away from attaining the "fairy tale" existence that the reader wants for her? Is there really such a thing as a "fairy tale" existence?

7. This book has an undefined ending, leaving the reader to draw his/her own conclusions. What do you think the future holds for Emilie

and the other characters?

8. Book covers introduce the body of work contained therein. What story clues can you find in this artistic design?

9. This is the author's second book in a series about self-determined young women coming of age after making unconventional decisions. What traits do Emilie from *Restless* and Edie from *Room Service Please* share? What messages do you think the author wants to convey to her audience?

Read on for an excerpt from
ROOM SERVICE PLEASE

Gold and Silver Award Winner
The BookFest

Room Service Please

Prologue

Sometime in that moment when life takes your hand and ushers you through a door, the door revolves, your hand gets pulled, and you step eagerly into an unknown. I won't say that this motion is an easy one, but one to behold for it happens to us all. We go through this door ushered in by only our absurd sense of self, our darn attitude, and our attempt at something reasonable, yet uncertain.

This was the way things were on the night of my sixteenth birthday. I never saw the door opening. I might have at one time seen only its closing, but once I stepped through that revolving door and into the Waldorf-Astoria Hotel foyer, I saw only opportunity. I was led from one realm and into another, and unbeknownst to me, ushered through one happy accident after another. Of course I knew nothing about hotels or foyers or steps that would take me across one room and into another. I knew nothing about men. I had only an idea of what they should be: attentive, passionate, eager.

Such naiveté. I use these words now, six years later, and laugh. Men are none of these things as they are all of them. They are absurd creatures I have come to appreciate. They are not easy to understand, but that is on me. I must continue to turn, to revolve, to look past obstacles that once stood before me and walk through new doors. I am a dancer. I dance. I feel certain that I will dance my way through this life easily putting one foot in front of the other, but I was not always this way. Where once I stumbled, I can now say I understand what it takes to high-step one's way through closed doors and accept the inevitable. Life is what we take, but more than that, life is what we are shown. It is on us to accept this. Or not.

I

June 18th 1922

Sunday mornings in New York City are placid. The night slips easily away to that rush of morning chill when inattentive minds awake slowly. There is motion in the street, but there is nothing to discern about the noise. These are the sounds one becomes accustomed to. They are nothing special. Nothing worth telling. Nothing. Does nothing have a sound? And if you were to describe nothing what words would you use?

Nothing should be black space. Emptiness. Regret. These words are necessary when describing the sound of nothing. But because my nothing once bore into me the way metal grinds on asphalt, my nothing was trolley wheels on a battered, slipshod rail. The shout of one lonely woman into the vestibule of the Waldorf-Astoria Hotel and the echo of her own voice returning to her. I couldn't understand what she was saying, but because there was nothing worth knowing about her, I turned to look out the hotel window just to be sure that nothing had not been superseded by something.

I had nowhere to go. I could have returned home, but that required taxi fare I did not have. My party shoes were soiled, my legs tired from dancing, and I did not have a penny to my name to call my ma. There was nothing to do but wait. I would wait until the empty street began to fill again or some bigger nothing swallowed me whole.

I hadn't a care in the world. Or did I? You will want to know why I was in the Waldorf-Astoria Hotel in the wee hours of the morning. I should tell you that turning sixteen is complicated. Or perhaps you already know? You will know what I know. Feel what I once felt, grumbling and complaining in all the right places to let your ma know just how miserable your life really is. But then what? You turn sixteen, in a confectionary, on a dance floor, in a hotel foyer, in a gentleman's room. With a chaperone or without one. Let me think just how I will share with you what might have been the most unrehearsed night of my life.

<>

It was on the eve of my sixteenth birthday when, against all reason, Ma bought me a pair of head-turning party shoes. She pulled at a snag in her limp stocking, took a long look at me in those caramel-colored heeled slippers, ostentatiously adorned with large satin bows, and threw away caution. I saw the wheels in her mind turn the way a worn handle turns on a meat grinder pushing blood into a vice. She was once young, I reasoned, wanting something like a pair of new shoes. Hadn't she told me all those stories of Jersey City, and want? I didn't grow up to put my head down and walk in shoes not destined for me, I told her, but my ma, my God-has-plans-for-us ma, will always see the world differently.

Ma took the money she was saving for someone, God, I guess, and pushed those hard-earned pennies across a dime-store counter with the hope only a desperate mother could muster. I was going to be escorted to the Waldorf-Astoria Hotel confectionary, a highfalutin place where the rich rub shoulders with the rich, and where someone like me would need to hitch a ride on the coattails of someone like Charlie Harrison to be allowed inside. So to her this was going to be money well spent. The shoes hurt the minute I put them on. They were tight in the toe box, and too short for my still-growing feet. But these were the ones she wanted for me, so I slipped on the party shoes, and with that tossed aside every ounce of good sense my mother ever wished she had given me. She had plans. We both had plans. In New York City.

New York City has run its course. Every bit of it will one day decay back into the rotten ground from whence it came two-bit brick by two-bit brick. I wish I'd known yesterday what I knew today. That all good girls, who once hoped and dreamt big, knew that a thing hoped for diminishes before your very eyes the moment it is wished for, and that anything worth having should be appreciated for what it is. Sixteen years didn't teach me the ways of the world. I knew better than to pin my hopes on days that might not come, and this is why I felt my birthday night was mine to do with as I wished. It was mine, after all. Wasn't it? Moments seized become experiences that no one can take from you, and overlooked shoes sitting in a dusty torn box on a dime-store shelf only become undervalued if forgotten. If Ma thought this she didn't say.

I hated those new shoes. I wouldn't tell Ma this. I would tell her that I really was the envy, because I was. That the shoes helped me dance the best, because they did. That the wine stains would come out easily. That this was arguably the happiest sixteenth birthday party a girl has ever had. I would share only the details of the night that she would understand: that orchids die, that soda drinks get spiked, and that curls fall. I wouldn't tell her that Charlie couldn't be responsible for me. She would never have agreed, but that down-on-his-luck Charlie wasn't capable of accompanying a sixteen-year-old girl, on the verge of becoming a woman, to a hotel candy counter. He was just a boy.

I turned images from the night before over in my mind like the clattering wheel, the worn handle, and the memory began to sharpen as the champagne fog lifted. There was a pair of unwanted shoes, a missing pair of perspiration-stained white gloves, and a torn frock. I lay down uneasily on an aging settee in a hotel foyer too tangled to move. There was a dark-haired man, not Charlie, lying in a tousled bed upstairs too drunk to know who spent the night with him, but I knew. The wheel continued to grind. My mind returned to the dark-paneled room and to the sun-kissed man.

Sunlight awakened sooty glass panes as it streamed through the oversized arched windows into the hotel foyer and made elongated geometric patterns on the black-and-white tiled floor. I tucked my swollen feet under me, curled up into a ball, and closed my eyes so that I could see more clearly. A mother should be out looking for her daughter when she realizes she has not come home, but only if she is your ma. My ma would not be out searching near empty streets, under-lit alleyways, nor rain-swollen gutters. She would not frantically inquire about me by telephone, or telegram, or by some desperate knock on a stranger's door simply because she trusted Charlie, Charlie's pedigree, and Charlie's overpriced orchid corsage.

If I tell you how Charlie Harrison, of all people, wound up bringing me to my destiny on the night of my sixteenth birthday, June 17, 1922, will you promise me you will take off your ill-fitting shoes and pull up a chair? I have one for the story books. Charlies are a dime a dozen and men like the one in the corner suite deserve recognition and to have their stories told. Not because they seduce, and can make a young girl's life a living hell if she winds up pregnant and thrown out onto the street, but because dapper men in the very prime of their life, like the expensive-looking man from the upstairs apartment, see only nothing in a world too blinded by nothings, and are wanting something. Like me.

Continue reading
Room Service Please by Alicia Cahalane Lewis

tatteredscript.com

CPSIA information can be obtained
at www.ICGtesting.com
Printed in the USA
JSHW041455020423
39282JS00007B/18/J